THE NOVELTY HAS WORN OFF

Fambles – Year 3
Anthology For 2021

CONTENTS

Paul Magrs 1
  Isle of Cats 1
  The Arse in the Sky 11
  The Awful Thing in the Road 16
  The Cheese Pirates 20
  The Hill 24
  The Launderette Stories 29
  When the Sky Fell In 34
Jeremy Hoad 37
  Who do I ask now? 39
  Going 41
  Your call is important to us 43
  35 Things About You 46
  Admitted 48
  My Mother's house 52
  That Biba Dress 54
  In The Supermarket 55
  Making Things Nice 57
Rylan John Cavell 59
  Will o' the Wisp 62
  The Toy Hospital – an excerpt 70

David Richards 95
   Witch Hunters 98
   Who You Gonna Call? 107
   Jumble 116
About the Authors 136

PAUL MAGRS

ISLE OF CATS

This story concerns a castaway in the eighteenth century, a man called Eddie, who was once on a ship en route to Southern Italy. The wooden ship he was on went down in a sudden storm in the middle of the night and the first thing Eddie really knew about it was that he was waking up on a beach on an island somewhere he had no idea where. Eddie was soaked to the skin, he was battered and bruised and he was completely alone.

Took him some time to fathom the news. He was the sole survivor of the wreck. Providence had marked him out for some reason. Even he couldn't see what made him so special that he'd be spared and the rest of those sailors and travellers had been doomed.

The island was sunny and hot and really... quite lovely, but Eddie was incapable of appreciating that at first.

Oh, but it was also the Isle of Cats.

And the first inkling Eddie had of that was as he lay there on the damp sand, just about dead and staring up at the sky... when the first of the cats padded across the beach towards him – curiously mewing – and they jumped on him and sat on his chest.

Eddie screamed. 'They'll eat me alive! They'll scratch out my eyes and make delicacies of them.'

But the wild cats of cat island did no such thing. They simply stared into Eddie's face. Their expressions gave nothing away.

They simply went: 'Mew mew. Mew mew. Weeee-oooooo.'

The three were joined by another two. These sat upon Eddie too.

'Weeeoooooo. Unngow. Mew mew.'

'Uhhh....' Eddie tried to speak. To tell them they were getting heavy, and noisy.

More and more cats, alerted by the excited fracas on the shore, came slinking out of the jungle to see what all the commotion was.

'Wooo wooo! Wee-ooo! Look what we've got!'

Cats of all different colour and stripe and size. Cats with one single intent, it seemed.

To sit on the castaway.

Mind, they dried out his waterlogged clothes quite quickly, as a result. And, after several hours of sitting on him, they let him get up and stagger into the forest of his new island home.

But they followed him.

THE NOVELTY HAS WORN OFF

And other cats came creeping out of the undergrowth and they kept an eye on him, too.

They were devoted to him. They loved to watch every little thing he did, those cats.

Eddie picked exotic fruit and chopped it up and ate it. He drank from a cool pond in the forest glade. He swam and washed under a waterfall. Then he built a little shelter under wide and fleshy leaves.

And all the cats jumped on him like a great, twisty, living blanket. They purred loudly on top of him as he tried to sleep.

'Oh, cats, cats, you're lovely, and I know you mean me no harm. But go and sleep somewhere else. You can stay close by. But you don't have to lie on top of me, do you? Not all of you, surely?'

But the cats affected not to understand a word of this. And they carried on lying bonily and furrily on top of their new Cat King. They even took it in shifts – with oddly rare cooperative turn-taking – to make sure that everyone got a turn at lying on Eddie.

Some of them came to stare straight into his face. Some of them loved to try to push their claws and paws into his mouth, or to boop him on the nose.

'Yes, yes, lovely,' said Eddie diplomatically. But he wished they could leave him alone for just a while.

In the daytimes he could escape from their attentions by moving about. But as soon as he sat down – wherever he was on the Isle of Cats – whamm!! He'd have one cat two cat three cats sitting upon his lap.

Soon it just became his way of life.

Eventually it was like he couldn't remember a time when his every hour wasn't plagued by this feline insistence.

* * *

Years passed. Years and years. And it was like Eddie forgot who he was supposed to be.

Until...

Another wooden ship came sailing by. It was looking for precious cargo that had been lost on the first. The ship's captain spotted the island from afar and, as his bark approached, he noted the plume of smoke. On the island Eddie was having a barbecue of wild rabbits and birds and he was turning the spit as all his cat friends looked on hungrily, with avid, drooling stares.

This jamboree in paradise was interrupted by the arrival of Captain Curdle and his sailors, who came ashore with treasure on their minds.

THE NOVELTY HAS WORN OFF

But all they found was one wild and hairy man who had a lot of catty friends.

Now, afterwards, Eddie could not quite reconstruct the order of events. He and his friends were horrified by the advent of these piratical gentleman who came wading ashore from the ramshackle Quattro Formaggio. He could recall Captain Curdle's hideous disappointment that there were no riches to be found here on the island. No washed up-treasure trove. No chest of glittering jewels. Just this man. A man who could barely talk the King's English anymore. Mostly he went 'mew mew mew' and 'ungow!'

The worst thing Eddie could remember was that they took him away from his friends.

The pirates stamped and shouted and they waved blazing torches. They shot blunderbusses into the air, making parrots shriek and animals gibber. And all the cats hissed and screeched and went running into the trees.

'No..! No..! Come back... come back, my friends..!' cried Eddie.

But Captain Curdle's men took hold of the skinny castaway and dragged him off.

Their reasoning being that he seemed to be the only surviving relic of the ship that had gone down. Perhaps someone in England would be prepared to pay a reward for him? This unpromising hairy man was all the treasure they were likely to find on the Isle of Cats...

So they took Eddie aboard the tender, all tied up, and rowed him out to the Quattro Formaggio. And all the way there he struggled and screamed in protest. The island receded behind them and he sobbed and couldn't stop staring at it.

Then they clapped him in irons and gagged him and put him in the brig aboard the pirate ship, and forgot about him, mostly, as they took the long route back to Britain.

The men of the Quattro Formaggio met with many more adventures over the next few months. All kinds of adventures. Cheesy ones, mostly.

But at last they sailed back into port. Back to London, where all were wanted men, and it was all a bit dicey.

They dragged Eddie out into the smoky city and he blinked at the pearlescent skies and coughed at the heavy and sulphurous air. This wasn't his island paradise. This place stirred memories deep inside him, but not happy ones. He wasn't where he wanted to be.

The pirates were intent on getting a good price for this man they had cared for and brought all this way across the seas... and – miraculously! – they managed to reunite him with a surviving relative.

THE NOVELTY HAS WORN OFF

Eddie's sister – Louella Armstrong – was a mature woman whose husband was in the shipping business. They lived in a tall townhouse on Baker Street, quite close to the entrance to Regent's Park. Lou wept and brayed with noisy relief that her little brother had been brought back to her, and she installed him in a bedroom in the attic of their home.

Her husband wasn't so keen. He didn't like the wild look in Eddie's eye, nor the way that he had forgotten most of his English and his human manners. But Lou was indulgent, feeling sure that just a bit of home-cooking and the lovely warmth of a family home would bring her brother back to civilisation.

He lay in his bunk at the top of the house with the windows open. The swirling scents of spring came into the room.

And also, the noisy brouhaha from London Zoo.

He could hear... the animals.

Specifically, the lions and tigers and pumas and leopards.

And they were calling out to him.

Eddie half-clambered out of the attic window and called out across the rooftops: 'I'm here! My friends! I'm here! Look here!'

Down on Baker Street little domestic cats, trotting back and forth about their daily tasks, took note and looked with interest up at the wild man hanging out of the attic.

When the maid opened the door next, several cats flew in past her. 'What? *What?*' she wailed, hardly realising what was going on.

'Weee-ooo! Weee-ooo!' shouted the Baker Street moggies. 'Mew mew! Mew mew!'

Up they thundered, up the stairs. Up three flights of stairs, four flights of stairs, right to the very top, and the attic, where Eddie was waiting for them.

'Ungow! Ungow! Ungow!' they all shouted.

And way across the green expanse of Regent's Park, the lions and tigers roared their approval.

That night, when Eddie lay in his bunk, absolutely covered in Baker Street cats who absolutely refused to leave, the big cats broke out of London Zoo. Under cover of darkness they slunk past the duckpond and through the iron gates. They knocked down the front door and flew up the stairs…

All to see Eddie.

Who was delighted, in turn, to see them.

'But why do you do it?' they were asked again and again, by the servants, the family, the newspapermen and the experts who came to look at this funny going on. 'Why would you go out of your way, all of you? Simply to lie on top of Eddie in the night? What's so great about Eddie..?'

THE NOVELTY HAS WORN OFF

The cats glanced at each other and shrugged and mostly disdained to answer such a dull set of questions. Why did they have to explain anything to humans?

But it was the lion who shook his mane and roared sighingly and yawned and took it upon himself to answer for the whole lot of them. 'We just like him, that's all.'

Fambles – Year 3 Anthology For 2021

THE NOVELTY HAS WORN OFF

THE ARSE IN THE SKY

I was there the very moment that it arrived.

I know that many millions of people saw it that day – all over the Earth – but I was one of those who just happened to be looking up at the very instant that it entered the whatsitcalled.

The stratosphere? The upper atmosphere?

The sky.

Yes, I was staring up at the massing, unfriendly clouds of January – it was the crack of dawn – and I was witness to the arrival of that vast, bulbous, alien object in all our lives. The inexplicable fundament of the air.

That morning I was at an early book sale in a shady back alley in Islington. These makeshift markets were a regular occurrence and the cognoscenti would gather furiously around brimming tea chests and cardboard boxes and tarpaulins spread out on the cobbles. We would be shuffling and rummaging through thousands of shabby volumes, each one of us avid for that rare first edition, that unexpected oddity still in its dust wrapper, or that surprise bargain that would fill an aching corner in our personal bookish hoard.

Very rarely did any of us look up from the shifting mounds of hardbacks and paperbacks in that alleyway. I happened to have a crick in my neck from repeated nights of falling asleep while reading. I also had need of a bloody good sneeze from all the paper dust I was inhaling. That's why I was looking up at that particular moment and I caught the very first glimpse of the apparition.

Pale, pinkish, orangey-blue. Slightly downy like a vast, unholy nectarine. Glowing in the pearlescent light of near dawn. It consisted of two gigantic fleshy globes squeezed together as if in a concentrated frown. Almost disapproving of the teeming life it surveyed as it hovered high above the metropolis.

It was the arse from outer space.

* * *

Strange to think back now, about it being a shocking thing, when we've all become rather used to its baleful presence, hovering over us at all hours of the day: silent, impassive, mysterious. Queer to imagine a time before its advent; before news of its arrival spread far and wide.

It's been almost eleven months since it manifested itself far above our heads and entered our consciousness like the crack of doom. The news services and the television stations have never stopped

THE NOVELTY HAS WORN OFF

going crazy over it. After all these months we've never stopped talking about it or speculating about its origin or purpose. We've certainly never begun to take that arse for granted.

It just sort of hangs there: disembodied, calm and rather moonlike.

It's as if it's watching us, I often think. Judging us.

The air force naturally sent fighter jets up there as soon as they could. Surveying the fleshy mass, making sure it posed no threat to life on Earth. They took photos and we all pored over these when they were reproduced in the papers and magazines. Dimpled, fuzzy. No legs, no torso, no other parts of the body. Just a vast human bum. Two buttocks floating squashily in the sky.

One of those planes flew slightly too close. His idea was to get a good look at the anus, hoping to scry some secret knowledge no one else had been privy to thus far. The pilot flew too close to the anomaly and he returned to Earth a gibbering wreck. Brave, foolish Icarus never recovered his wits, nor could tell us what he had seen up there.

No one else would fly that near, and so we have learned little more.

Satellites have taken pictures and all kinds of readings analysed the arse from every angle. Scientists have peered through their telescopes, trying to penetrate the ineffable mystery of the bottom in the sky.

All to no avail.

In just eleven months various cults have sprang up, with depressing inevitability.

'Is this the asshole of God?' they ask. 'Is this the Bumhole Divine?'

Cowled monks and new age crazies stand in open spaces staring up at the thing. Imploring it to communicate with them. Begging it to show them a sign. They flagellate themselves and light candles and sing songs to the giant arse. Once I observed a curiously moving ritual when they interrupted traffic on Tower Bridge and, acting as one, bared their own arses to the sky. I'm not sure what they were expecting to happen that lunch time in May, following their act of supplication, but absolutely bugger all did.

'Oh, Holy Arse in the sky,' they cry. 'Show us your will. Demonstrate the way we must go!'

But the arse remains inscrutable…

At least it has till now.

Madmen have used it as an excuse for various atrocities this year. 'The arse spoke to me in my dreams,' they gibber. 'The arse in the sky is manipulating me! It controls my emotions and my actions!'

THE NOVELTY HAS WORN OFF

There were cartoons, comic sketches, popular songs, even a full-length stage musical about the massive celestial arsehole during the course of the year. It had fully entered public consciousness, even before it had done very much at all.

The government told us they were being guided by the very best scientific advice over what to do about the giant arse.

There was a kind of stand-off. Earth. The arse. And nothing going on. Implacable. Impassive. An ominous silence.

And then...

Quite suddenly, eleven months since its manifestation above our heads, on a crisp and colourful autumn morning...

The floating arsehole did something extraordinary.

Once again I just happened to be in the right place at the right time to witness history.

At first it was hard to comprehend what I was actually seeing on that bright October morning, as the giant arse opened up just a tiny little bit and that dreadful darkness gazed down...

THE AWFUL THING IN THE ROAD

I looked out of our front window and that's when I saw the embarrassing thing in the road.

What on earth was it? And how had it got there?

Surely no one had put it there on purpose?

The bin men had been doing their rounds early that morning, waking us all up with the lorry and the trundling of the bins. Maybe this awful thing had fallen out of someone's wheelie bin and been left behind?

I suppose the bin men hadn't noticed it had slipped out and fallen into the road. Or maybe they had… and none of them had wanted to pick it up? Even with those heavy duty gloves they have to wear?

I don't blame them. Who knows where the awful thing had been?

And so it lay there on the damp tarmac. This thing that everyone was so deeply embarrassed about. No one came to claim it.

As that day went by old ladies ambled past in pairs, tutting when they saw it and then looking away. A drunk scowled at it, thinking he was imagining things. Children pointed and giggled, and one dared another to go and kick it. No, pick it up and chuck it at someone! But they didn't dare. They ran away, in fits of laughter about the awful thing in the road.

THE NOVELTY HAS WORN OFF

A dog crept up and gave it a cautious sniff. He hurried away.

Our street has a bend in it, so that people and cars coming round the corner couldn't see the dreadful thing until they were almost on top of it. Our upstairs window at the front of the house was a great vantage point for watching these moments of confrontation. I'm afraid I laughed. Aaarggh!! Look at that! In the road! Is that real? Is it really what I think it is? Who put that there? How disgusting!

I think it was there by accident. I don't think there was any malice in its appearance. I don't think any harm was meant by it. It had simply dropped out during its discreet journey via wheelie bin to the council van. But now here it was, in full public view.

Fancifully, I imagined how it must be feeling, the awful thing. So ashamed and helpless, I should think! It could hardly crawl away to safety and obscurity, could it?

The rain fell down. Drumming down for hours like it often does on our town. I think we all hoped that the rain would wash the thing away.

But when the sun came out the awful thing was still there.

Who was going to take responsibility for it? Who would don rubber gloves, and in front of the whole street, dispose of it safely?

But no one did.

Snow fell lightly and then more heavily and then the ground frosted over. The awful thing was stuck to the road. It wasn't going anywhere.

THE NOVELTY HAS WORN OFF

THE CHEESE PIRATES

I wanted to tell the story of the Cheese Pirates, and their dreadful, heartless leader, Captain Curdle. The whole thing turns my stomach and makes me queasy. But I'll try anyway.

He had a fondue fork for a right hand, you know. It came in handy for toasting things – marshmallows and bread... but it was even handier for sticking in the guts of his enemies! And for plucking out their organs like a nasty little grabber!

He was a terrible man, Captain Curdle. He was like a scourge of the seven cheese. I mean, seven *seas*.

His ship was old and hardy and rickety round the edges: The Quattro Formaggio.

Sailors would glimpse it on the horizon and an awful fear would grip their vitals. Oh no! Not the Quattro Formaggio...!

There'd be a whiff...

An increasingly strong odour...

It would come wafting across the choppy waves...

A persistent pong of greenish mildew and mould...

And they would know, those sailors. Terror would grip their entrails!

Captain Curdle and his crew were on their way!

THE NOVELTY HAS WORN OFF

* * *

How did they come to be like this? How did they first set sail?

What's the fiendish backstory of Captain Curdle and his crew of cutthroat curs?

Well, for a start, they were all milkmen.

They delivered milk in bottles, door to door, and they rode around the streets on milk floats. Up at the crack of dawn and running about. Each of them had very large hands, able to carry ten pints all at once.

Except for Captain Curdle, who lost one of his hands (Did you hear that tale? About the Crocodile? It wasn't a crocodile, it was someone's Alsatian. CHOMP.) When his hand was replaced by a fondue fork, his days as a milkman were numbered).

He went rogue. He went off to sea, stealing all the dairy products from his float. Bobbing along on the briny with the milk and eggs and butter and cheese. Lots and lots of glorious cheese. He had so much he hardly knew what to do with it, so he threw a fondue party for his fellow milkmen.

'We could all go rogue,' he shrugged, affecting nonchalance. 'What do you fellas think? We could all become pirates.'

'Cheese Pirates!' all the milkmen cheered. 'Why not?'

And they toasted their new vocation, and all the filthy fun they'd have, with cheese on toast and just a splash of Worcester sauce.

THE NOVELTY HAS WORN OFF

THE HILL

We're all going over the hill!

There was talk of going round it, so we could see what's on the other side, but apparently that's not doable. (I'm not clear on why exactly, but anyway.)

So – we're all going over the hill!

It's quite a journey, by all accounts! A really arduous yomp! Various reports have come back from others over the years. Some have found themselves in real trouble. Some wore themselves out. Some couldn't stop bickering amongst themselves. Some of them only got halfway up and then they suddenly went quiet.

A few baulked at the very idea of having to go over the hill.

Why can't we go under? Why can't we fly?

Well, we can't. We have to face facts. We have to go over, step by step.

There's no doubt about that. No wriggle-room, when it comes to going over the hill.

The weather is unpredictable and it's foggy much of the time, so you can barely see the peak anyway.

Some people say: Is there even a top of the hill to go over? Can you see it? Prove it to me! Show me it's worth it!

THE NOVELTY HAS WORN OFF

Well, you have to crane your neck. Squint a bit. Have a look at the scrappy maps and charts other people have left behind.

There!

Sometimes on clear and brilliant days, or by the light of the moon or in the middle of a savage lightning storm – that's when you see the top.

Oh crumbs. Quite a long way up, eh?

Quite perilous-looking. Impressive, really.

All that way!

We've got all that way to go!

So make sure you pick your companions well. No one you can't abide, obviously. No one who's going to chuck you down a crevasse. Or elbow sharply past you in their own rush to the top. Or nick your precious supplies. Or chunter on endlessly as you toil your way up.

Remember – don't pack too much stuff. You have to carry all that gubbins with you. And there's no wi-fi up there, or anything to connect to, and no sockets to plug chargers into.

You might think you can get your friends to carry your bags for you. Some do. Don't be soft and go round offering to carry everyone else's nicknacks. Some folk will take a lend. Just look at them! Bombing ahead! Galloping up the winding path! They're not looking back… and meanwhile you've got all the rucksacks –

crammed packed with all their crap and dirty pants and socks and all kinds of horrible things. Typical!

So...

DON'T stop for breathers so long that you lose your nerve. DON'T let yourself get vertigo as you try to enjoy the vista on the less misty days. DON'T get drawn in by the weird, yelping siren song of the yeti. Oh, yes – he's up there somewhere. That furry get! You know, he EATS unwary travellers! You'll come across his abominable footprints and they'll make you shudder with dread and wonder. But hurry on by!

So here we go.

We're all going over the hill!

There's no way round it. There's no avoiding it.

The air's a bit thinner as you get higher up. Breathe carefully...

Look, maybe I'm dwelling on the negatives a bit much?

Let's think ourselves lucky!

Yes, it's tough. It's not for softies.

But just think.

Think about drinking hot sweet coffee out of a flask and seeing that view. The whole world comes swimming into focus!

Think about having lovely companions with you all that way and the whole world opening up around you.

Just think how it must look from the top!

THE NOVELTY HAS WORN OFF

And they say – from up there – that's when you see what's down the other side. That's got to be worth it, hasn't it?

Personally I think it's probably more of the same. I kind of hope it is.

(But it might just be a vertiginous wasteland of yeti crap. Stinky and all downhill. That would be a disappointment, I guess.)

Whatever – we're all going over the hill – together!

And at least we don't have to do it on our own.

And who knows? We might even have a laugh.

Fambles – Year 3 Anthology For 2021

THE LAUNDERETTE STORIES

Many of my earliest stories were written at the end of the nineteen-eighties in a launderette. That's where I met the Tiger Woman and I wish I could remember what her story was about. What did she say to the Me character in that story? What was the thing that made me want to write it down? And what made me call her the Tiger Woman anyway?

She was like a vagrant, shuffling in, a great big mound of old clothes on a trolley. Wedging her behind into the doorway, coming in backwards. Bringing in a great waft of filthy air with the autumn breeze. Stealing away the comforting warmth and the flowery detergent smells and fabric conditioner hum of the launderette.

The fur coat she wore wasn't really from a tiger, and there weren't sharp claws at the ends of the sleeves. That was something I made up for the story, and I've no idea why. She came and sat by me and the coat was still full of chilly rain. She was sprinkling us all with rain as she settled.

Then she started talking and... and I wish I could remember what the Tiger Woman said.

I want to think that it had something to do with Nightingale Farm, the abattoir at the top of the hill, that smelled so horrible. The whole town reeked of maggots and corruption. I like to think of her avenging all those dead animals somehow.

I want to think I made her a were-tiger in my story. A real tiger woman, who transformed by moonlight from bag lady into monster.

I want to think that I made her a kind of femme fatale from the 1940s in a long-ago backstory and now, fallen on hard times, she recalls her glory days.

Any of those stories were ones I might have knocked together as I doodled and noodled in that notebook of mine. (Half the pages empty, half of them lined, just as I liked it.)

I carried on writing it all down as soon as I was home in my student attic, after I lugged my bag of warm washing back up the hill. I couldn't resist turning her straight into a story. I had met a character! A ready-made character! And she had told me so much... about... about...

It took at least two hours in those launderettes. The huge drums of the driers going round and round. The juddering washers shaking together, squeezed up along the front window, shuddering in a line like they were suppressing giggles.

I sat with my messy notebook and just wrote and wrote. As I waited for machines to come free, I wrote stuff down. My attention wandered. One story bled into another. Drawings and scribbles and doodles as I

THE NOVELTY HAS WORN OFF

idly watched the other washers. Those untangling their smalls and pulling their sleeves inside out. Those who were folding everything so tidily and those who emptied out funky-smelling bin bags.

Me and the Tiger Woman sat there watching them all and sharing my cigarettes.

And she told me stuff. About her own life, and the people who came in. She sat here every day even though she never washed anything. She just picked up the bits and pieces left behind and added them to her collection in her trolley. Heavier by the day, it was tougher to pull it up that steep hill in the student part of town. She huffed and puffed more each time I saw her.

I wonder why I called her the Tiger Woman? I wonder what it was she told me?

I lost that book of scribbles and stories. One of many books I lost over the years. I didn't get obsessed with keeping hold of all those things until I was older, and realised that I'd forget and lose the thread if I lost things or gave them away...

The Tiger Woman from the Lancaster launderette vanished with that book of stories and scribbles. I'm reaching for her now, and trying to draw her into this book. But not every character will come when they're called.

She grunts, gets up, nudges her wire trolley full of bits of other people's outfits closer to the door. The autumn wind's picked up and it's coming on sleet. She waves a brief goodbye and lurches out.

THE NOVELTY HAS WORN OFF

Fambles – Year 3 Anthology For 2021

WHEN THE SKY FELL IN

Yesterday I read that folk tales have been used for a very long time for all kinds of reasons. One of their many uses has been for making fun of 'mass hysteria', 'mayhem' and 'paranoia.' Fancy that!

This is where Chicken Licken comes in. (I much prefer our name to the American version. Henny Penny sounds unnecessarily fussy somehow.)
Remember that story?

The sky's gonna come falling in! Running around like crazy warning everyone. It's the end of the world! Duck and cover! Protect and survive! Dashing about the farmyard like a headless chicken.

In the current catastrophe I'm pleased to say that there's been rather less panic than you might expect.

Chicken Licken has resorted to Twitter mostly, spreading every conspiracy theory he can find, raging about fake news and quibbling with almost everything he reads in 'the mainstream media.'

Cocky Locky has taken up baking, with mixed results.

THE NOVELTY HAS WORN OFF

Ducky Lucky is livestreaming her keep-fit classes, flapping up and down and keeping everyone trim. She's hoping for a medal in the New Year Honours. Dame Ducky would suit her, she says.

Goosey Loosey has waddled round the farmyard ten thousand times but forgot to ask anyone to sponsor her first. Home-schooling for her goslings has flown out of the window.

Turkey Lurkey deeply regrets the loosening of restrictions at Christmas time. He'd have been happier if the festive season had just been cancelled altogether.

Foxy Loxy is self-isolating. He hasn't any symptoms, he's just had enough of all those crazy birds.

Chicken Licken would like to add: 'Don't worry! Don't panic! It's not the end of the world after all. We'll get through this! We can do it! You'll see..!'

Fambles – Year 3 Anthology For 2021

JEREMY HOAD

We have all needed support and friendship during the pandemic and Fambles has provided that for me creatively. It is a place to test things out, to discuss things openly, to explore ideas and express opinions both on the work we share and on life generally.

The poems here are not what I was going to include because everything changed. The first reflects on my Father's death over a decade ago and the others follow my Mother's death very recently. Eighteen months of resilience through the pandemic and then gone in a couple of weeks. I am grateful to the members of Fambles for their patience and understanding and the delay in publication this year as I reworked my contribution. Thank you to Paul. Above all thank you to my parents, Peter and Rita.

Fambles – Year 3 Anthology For 2021

THE NOVELTY HAS WORN OFF

WHO DO I ASK NOW?

Who do I ask now you're not here?
You always knew.
Those practical manly tasks around the house.
Plastering, plumbing, electrics.
You could tell me how to do things.
You knew how to do things
as well as how to not do things
and what to avoid.

Skills I remember you showing me.
Practicing how to shake hands.
Now there are only memories
and your dressing gown
hanging on the back of the bathroom door.
Photos on the mantlepiece.
Your wallet in the desk
and your watch in the bedside table drawer.

Telling you a joke on the phone.
You clearly didn't really get it
but you were polite.
Later that night
when you couldn't sleep
you phoned me at two in the morning
just laughing down the phone.
Monkeys in the bath made you laugh.

I've never really grasped being a man.
I was and will always be your son.
More than a decade after you've gone
I still think of things to tell you.
Things that will make you laugh.
Asking your advice is no longer possible.
But you're still around.
With me and part of me.

When you died I wept.
Some people have a delayed reaction.
I didn't.
A lifetime of love hit me instantly.
That phone call.
Peter has died.
Fiddling with your belt in the hall.
Asking for help and getting frustrated.
"Give me a hand, lamb."
Then you just crumpled.
Decades of being together.
Who do we ask now?

THE NOVELTY HAS WORN OFF

GOING

You are going.
I know you are.
We've been told.
We don't know when
or how long it will take
but you're leaving us.

I don't know what to do.
I'm trying to keep things normal.
Trying to keep talking.
But you don't always know what day it is.
And last week when it was dark
Is it morning or evening?

I need you.
I want to remember things with you.
But you won't be able to.
Details and times and places
slipping away from us.
Things that you remember that I don't
will be gone.
Drifting off somewhere else.
Memories with nobody to remember them.

We are both afraid.
And we are both pretending.
We will do our best.
Together.
We will keep ourselves
and I will keep you
even when you don't know yourself.
Even when it is no longer you.
There will still be us.
Forever together as we drift apart.

THE NOVELTY HAS WORN OFF

YOUR CALL IS IMPORTANT TO US

Please say the person or service you need.
Speak clearly and slowly
"Ward 5"
Did you mean Ward 30, Ward 32, Ward 40, Ward 33, Ward 22?
"No. Ward 5."
Did you mean Ian Foyle?
"No."
Please wait to speak to an operator.
Cheery jazz music jars your ear.
"Hello. Can I help you?"
"Can you put me through to Ward 5 please?"
"Where?"
"In the hospital."
"Which hospital."
"This one."
You specify the hospital.
"Well, how are we supposed to know? We serve all of the area."
"How am I supposed to know that? I phoned the number given for the hospital."
"That's not our fault. I don't work for that hospital. I work for the NHS."
"How am I supposed to know that?"
"You called this number."

"I don't care. I am trying to speak to the Ward my Mother is on."
"Don't speak to me like that."
And the line goes dead.
Four attempts.
No luck.
The line goes dead each time.
It shouldn't be this hard but it is.

THE NOVELTY HAS WORN OFF

Fambles – Year 3 Anthology For 2021

35 THINGS ABOUT YOU

Golf
Johnny Mathis
Deep brown eyes
Ngaio Marsh
Turquoise Hillman Imp
Shirley Bassey
Soft skin
Curling
Women's Royal Voluntary Service
Orange lipstick
Knitting purple tank tops for my toys
Dean Martin
Marks and Spencer
Prison visiting
Raffles in Singapore
Carpet handbag
SSPCA
George Harrison
Opium perfume
The Godfather
Amber beads
Sheepskin hat
Samaritans
Portofino
Nancy Sinatra

THE NOVELTY HAS WORN OFF

Rose gold necklace
Netball
World Wildlife Fund
Herb Alpert
LS Lowry
Silver sequinned Biba dress
Arran
Yellow Citroen Dyane
Reading Ponder and William to me
and Staying 35

ADMITTED

You're in hospital
Weak but responding well
Rest and physio, they say
We've been here before
You remember, after your fall

You've tested positive
Transferred to another hospital at 5am
The other one is a clean hospital, they say
Just standard practice

A quiet day, mostly dozing
Talking to the Occupational Therapist about further adaptations at home
I make you laugh on the phone
You cough

You're coping well
They have you on antibiotics
It's fine, just a little oxygen
You do well with the strength tests

Sleeping mostly
They say they'd expect a better response by now
And ask how communicative you are usually

THE NOVELTY HAS WORN OFF

Can I come up, they ask?

Driving to see you
Flask tea and sandwiches in the car
Talking nonsense to distract ourselves
Lorries and darkness

The empty house
Expectation
Inevitability
Doing normal stuff

More driving
Getting lost on arrival at the hospital
Being misdirected and redirected inside
Finding your Ward

Mask
Apron
Gloves
Visor

Saying hello
Being cheerful
Telling you news
Talking about when you come home

Giving you water on a pink sponge
You mumble thank you
I know it's hard
Build up your strength

I'm here with you
I'll look after you
Everything is fine at home
People sending love

Driving
Visiting
Talking
Coping

Covid
Pulmonary Embolism
Pneumonia
Is there a Do Not Resuscitate in place?

You're not actively dying
But you're not responding to treatment
Stroking your hair
Blue gloves, grey hair

Holding your hand
The smell of sanitiser

THE NOVELTY HAS WORN OFF

Imagining your perfume
You're still there

Peeling back the blue film
Struggling with too small gloves
Steaming up and telling you that's the reason
I need to blow my nose

Withdrawal of treatment

I'm still talking
Saying I love you
Being there with you
You seem smaller

We don't need to talk now
We've said everything we need to
But I keep talking
Tears on my face

Your breathing has changed
I say you can go if you want to
Driving home

Two missed calls from the hospital

MY MOTHER'S HOUSE

The sound the door makes
The way the light falls
on the curtains
The paint wearing thin
on the bathroom radiator

My Mother isn't in her chair
It's now just a chair
still hers but not
She never liked it anyway

The drawing room that
became her bedroom
contains drinks parties with
my Father hovering in the door
Suddenly shy in company

The expectation hangs in every room
This is now a time capsule
thrown back from a mirror
Ready to be dismantled
Something I can't quite grasp

My Mother's house
is no longer hers

THE NOVELTY HAS WORN OFF

She is not here
It's just a building now
But every room holds her

THAT BIBA DRESS

That silver sequined Biba evening dress
you gave to the Amateur Dramatic Society
The one you wore with silver slingbacks
with an air of Shirley Bassey
swaying and sparkling as you danced
when I saw you through the bannister on the stairs
at one of your parties
Pyjamas and frazzles upstairs
Cinzano and nibbles downstairs
I was with you when you bought it
In the shop with metal palm trees
They cut it up
And used it for a Dame's dress
In their pantomime
It went from new to vintage
In your lifetime
And became the dress of a Dame
At the same time Shirley did

THE NOVELTY HAS WORN OFF

IN THE SUPERMARKET

Popped into the supermarket
Needed a few things
There was a man at the door
I had to wait while a child on a bike got out the way
Reversing inelegantly
He was holding an orange
The man, not the child
"Do you know what Dementia and an orange have in common?"
He looked at me expectantly
I couldn't get past
"No"
"Dementia sufferers lose the weight of an orange from their brain."
I paused.
"Not the best time"
I felt the emotion in my chest.
"My Mother has just died. She had Alzheimers."
"Well, you'll be glad to know..."
"Really?"
"There's new research..."
"Please stop."
"I think it's time to end the sales pitch"
He looked at me blankly
I walked past

Holding myself together
"Look at our website"
Not now, I thought
Not now.

THE NOVELTY HAS WORN OFF

MAKING THINGS NICE

I'm making things nice for you
Tidying round, wiping things down
Making sure the phone and remotes are in reach
Clearing out the fridge and freezer
Running the hoover round
I want you to be comfortable
Your shawl on your chair
We'll get things sorted
The cills on the conservatory need repainting
I'll do that next time I'm up
Add it to your list
But you can't
You won't be here
You're not here now
We arrived to an empty house
And we're leaving an empty house
"Can you pass me the paper?"
No, I can't.

Fambles – Year 3 Anthology For 2021

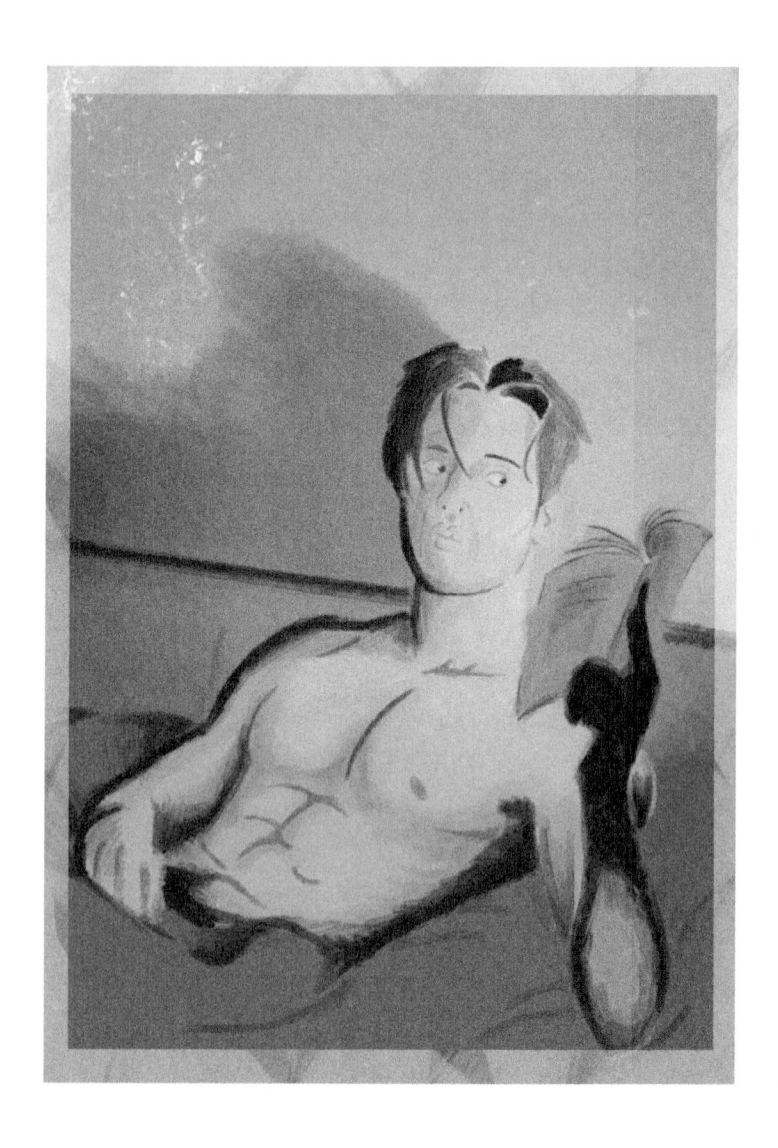

RYLAN JOHN CAVELL
The Year That Time Forgot

Someone recently asked me *'do you think anyone will actually remember this year, in five years time, and how awful and strange it has been?'* And my reply, after a thoughtful pause, was *'no!'*. I resolutely believe that 2020; the year of the zoom call, social distancing, wearing masks, and being forbidden to visit or to hug loved ones will be sponged from the collective memory of the world as quickly as can be managed. People won't want to remember!

But some people will. Some people have made it their mission to record, create, capture, and otherwise preserve a unique moment in our history; People like me, and the rest of Fambles. I refuse to forget how strange and isolating it was, even with my Johnny and Cheeto for company, how distant I suddenly felt from my friends and family. I channelled all that emotion and uncertainty into my creative work...

But something happened.

Fambles changed. For better or worse, it will be for time to test. The stresses of the year, and the societal upheavals that swept over the world threatened to shatter the 'no holds barred' arena of discourse that our group cherishes at its core. Personal issues, work commitments, and more have stolen away some of our number, but those of us that remain and attend regularly are all the more fired up with a drive to continue, and to help one another, and to challenge one another. After all, that's what Fambles is all about; a collective drive to better ourselves and one other.

THE NOVELTY HAS WORN OFF

WILL O' THE WISP

Sunday 15th August 2021

Listen. Shh. Listen. Do you hear it? A kind of jingling jangling swooshing sound that's almost like music? Shh, listen now! There! That's a *will o' the wisp*, and look, there, the tell-tail trail of light it leaves in its wake as it bobs and weaves and flutters about. They come and go as they please, do the will o' the wisps. Oh but this one looks a little sluggish, a little peaky. Shall we approach and see if it needs some assistance?

"Last night was an absolute hoot!" Says the wisp, in a nasal and drawn out little voice, "I think I'm still drunk."

It's 2 in the afternoon.

Shall we ask the wisp where he's been, and what he's seen? He's sure to regale us with wonderful stories of fairies and goblins and other such creatures from the World Next Door.

"You haven't any ibuprofen?" The wisp clutches my sleeve, it's pale eyes glittering like milky fireworks.

I haven't any such thing about my person.

"Bugger." Says the wisp.

"Where have you come from?" says I to the wisp, and he tells me.

THE NOVELTY HAS WORN OFF

"Levenshulme. Funny place. And were rainbows everywhere!"

I ask the wisp to tell me of this mythical, far-away land of rainbows, and the strange creatures that abode there.

"I've a migraine coming on." Says the wisp, before moving off to wail splashily behind a rhododendron bush. I await his return, whereupon he plonks himself down in the crook of a tree's roots, and waves me over with one delicate, translucent hand.

"Please tell me. Oh tell me, do!" I implore, "Tell me a tale of this magical realm of Levenshulme!"

"You won't leave me be until I've told you?" he asks.

I sit down cross legged in front of him, eager for the story.

He sighs, massaging his fingertips into the soft skin of his forehead, "Well..." He begins, "there was a poetry night with no poets... or was that no audience? No, there were definitely poets. Either way the people who read to one another had a lovely time. One of them was bouncing around like a puppy, full of the energy possessed solely my kids TV presenters."

"What's one of those?" I ask the wisp, but he doesn't hear me, lost as he is in his rememerences.

"Another read like he was trying to seduce the room, lots of words that were sultry and slow and sensory. Oh and there was a cabaret!"

"Whats one of those?" I ask, imagining some kind of carved wooden cabinet. Again the wisp, lost in his thoughts, doesn't hear me.

"The weirdest village fete I've ever been to." He mutters thoughtfully, continuing, "...there was another poet, done up like a gangster from the '20s, whose poems were ever so gynecological. They had lovely red shoes on. Lots of sexy poems about overly friendly ladies. Scandalous! I saw a fella clutching his pearls at least twice, while fluttering a fan to hide his jaw hanging open."

I chuckle a little at the way the wisp tells the story, and he looks at me with those large creamy, misty old eyes. Eyes that have seen a thousand years or more, through which I detect a strange and unfamiliar wisdom.

"Pardon me, dear." He says, rushing away to noisily visit the rhododendron once more. Presently he returns, wiping his mouth on the back of his hand, "There was clashing music, coming through walls from all over the place. Shirtless waiters here, their bodies all ripply and bulgy. Glitter encrusted Queens there, singing and swearing at people across noisy, dark rooms full of sweaty, cheering revellers."

THE NOVELTY HAS WORN OFF

"It all sounds ever so exotic!" I say breathily.

"It's not." the wisp raises his eyebrows meaningfully, "and that's why it was such fun. Oh, I've just remembered! Someone's wig flew off!"

"Is it a kind of bird?" I ask, and the wisp slaps me around the face.

"Oh do shut up! I'm suffering here, and you're holding me up in Doiley Wood longer than I usually care to linger. Let me get on!"

"Sorry." I nurse my cheek, baffled, and remain quiet then, keen to hear more.

"Where was I? See, you've made me forget what I was – oh yes the wig! There's that bit in the song, from that musical. You know the one? The one with all the funny dance moves? Well there was a room full of people dancing along, and at the end, like in the show, everyone falls down. Well one went down so hard their wig went sailing off through the crowd! I thought a wild animal had got in."

I nod, smiling, as it seems the right thing to do. But the story of the wisp contains so many references to the World Next Door, I find myself befuddled and vexed. But it is rare indeed to encounter a will o' the wisp, so I remain quietly sat in the soft earth beneath the tree, as he continues his saga.

"The dog show was adorable." the wisp cooes, "all those waggy tails and happy faces and boopable snoots. One of them chased me a bit, but I didn't mind."

The story unfolds in a rambling, divergent kind of way, moving from one thought to another as they come to him. He tells me about the Panda, the Cat, and the Dreadful Teddy. He tells me about the singer in a pretty red dress, her guitar bristling with tangled steel whiskers. He tells me about the singer, and the power cuts that amusingly interrupt everything. And he tells me about the Queens Who Eat Of No Animal, and their rollicking sing-along of everyone's favourite camp classics. I have no understanding of what any of these things are, but in the end I think he has enjoyed telling me about them. He sits back, smiling warmly, in the nook in the tree's roots.

"Now, if you'll excuse me, I need to get a Full English inside me, else I shan't recover. Toodle-oo!"

And with that the wisp flutters woozily away, bumping into a low branch and muttering foreign curses under his breath. The strange jingling, jangling, swooshing sounds that accompany his movements fade as he moves away. It sounds almost like music. Then he is gone, and I hurry home, as it is dangerous to be alone in the forest.

THE NOVELTY HAS WORN OFF

Fambles – Year 3 Anthology For 2021

THE NOVELTY HAS WORN OFF

THE TOY HOSPITAL - AN EXCERPT

A pug in a yellow anorak left a fluffy-tummy height trail in the snow as it trotted by its owner's side. At the entrance to a shabby little boutique with a lopsided window the pug cocked its leg.

"Get away with you. I'll have none of that on my doorstep, thank you." Said an ancient woman from the depths of a curly blue-rinsed up-do. She shooed the dog away with the stiff broom with which she was clearing the doorway. Sparkling clouds of frigid snow and ice swirled before her as she set vigorously to her work. The pug was ushered on, to toilette elsewhere.

Pausing briefly, she leaned on the shaft of the broom, and took in the picture-postcard scene. Thomas Street was usually buzzing with early morning coffee drinkers, business people yakking loudly into their newfangled mobile telephones, cyclists jostling for priority with taxis, and occasionally one or two sorry states still making their way home from the night before. Greta Pudding curiously examined the strange new sound that the snow storm had brought to Manchester; Silence.

From the front of her teetering establishment, she usually felt the world was at her doorstep. She loved the hurly-burly of city life, while maintaining her calm hurricane's eye. That eye was the shop whose doorstep she had paused the sweeping of. And it wasn't any old run-of-the-mill shop. It was a toy shop. But more than that, even. It was a toy hospital. She was very proud of the work she did within the dark and crooked walls of her establishment.

Today the world at her doorstep was held at arm's reach. It was just a hop further than she could make with her crunchy old knees. The streets of Manchester had been taken by surprise by the icy storm overnight. Gritters went out too late, doing only half a job before having to give up and take shelter. Blowing sideways, striking the city at acute angles from the nearby Pennines, the storm had sprung from nowhere, and when it was done, it went back off to nowhere. Roads were smothered. Pavements were coated. Doorways were inundated. A very odd snow-storm indeed; It had intention, and malice. It clawed at letterboxes, sanded sharp angles to pumice curves, and set with murderous intent at the statues and spires of the city skyline. The rattling of window panes had woken Greta and her business partner Sylvia Garland, who both dwelt above the shop. They had huddled together, basking in the warmth of the electric fire in their pokey living room, where they watched the blizzard attack the street. They heard at least one window break. Thankfully it wasn't one of their own. Sylvia felt the cold more acutely, despite being in possession of a sturdily padded frame. Like an old armchair, she was comfy and patterned and welcoming. Greta on the other hand was frail and spindly, and shorter by a head than her friend. Her joints protested like an old gate, and she was barbed as the rusted nails that held together her rickety frame.

"A very odd snow-storm indeed." Sylvia had said, as she pulled a blanket around her sturdy shoulders. Hot cocoa had soothed them, eventually, back to the land of nod.

From the doorstep, broom in hand, Greta examined the glistening white icing with a squint of her spectacled eyes. She was suspicious of it. The sweet confection of the day hid the grime, and the grey, and the red-brick dust belly of the beast. The sky was a pale blue dome, and entirely absent of clouds.

"A very odd snow-storm. Indeed." Intoned Greta, soaking up the silence.

Greta had not had an easy life. Troublesome people seemed drawn to her, and over the years she had grown a hard shell, like a wrinkled walnut, to keep herself safe. She had become known by some as a curmudgeon. By others a survivor. By some, in somewhat more unsavoury terms. But whatever they called her bothered her not one jot. She knew herself very well, and would not permit the opinion of others to dent her worth.

She made her way through the shop front of the Toy Hospital, admiring her handiwork. Rescued rocking horses galloped in still-life upon their curved rockers. Recombobulated puppets hung from their waxed strings, not a tangle in sight, and merry, with rosy painted cheeks. Teddies with paisley neckerchiefs, dollies that blinked when you laid them down, wind-up waddling ducks, and perfectly fitting nesting dolls. All of these and more adorned the rippling shelves fixed to the walls, and the atolls that sprung up here and there from the worn sea-blue carpet.

The only person in all her life who could see beyond that uncrackable exterior, and into the soft, squashy Victoria sponge that was truly Greta Pudding, was her life-long friend and business partner. Sylvia emerged from the little back room with a fresh pot of tea, and the pockets of her tabard stuffed with tiny tools. She tinkled and jingled as she walked. Sylvia was the nurse to Greta's doctor. But today there was no surgery planned. Still, Sylvia was prepared for an emergency. Eyes and noses and buttons could come away from old and much-loved cuddly toys at any moment! The Toy Hospital would always be ready.

"It's the first of December." Sylvia said. She attempted to sound casual. It was a significant date in both their lives, and never passed without incident.

"I'm aware." Greta clattered their chipped and familiar mugs from beside the mechanical cash register, and presented them, "and I'm gasping."

The tea was served with lemon and honey, and the two of them sipped in companionable silence.

"What'll it be this year?" Sylvia asked eventually.

Greta finished her tea and placed the mug down firmly as answer. No answer. They both knew what would happen that evening. Well, they had an inkling.

"Come along, Greta." Sylvia cooed, "We know what he's up to, after a fashion. If we put our heads together we can put a stop to it. Maybe not for good, but for today at least." Sylvia had always been the optimist of the two.

"Cats." Greta spat. "This year it'll be cats."

"So what do we do?"

"*We* do nothing." Greta scowled behind her oversized horn-rimmed glasses, "He's my itch to scratch. You just keep yourself cosy in your bed tonight. I'll deal with him."

Sylvia mushed her lips together in consternation. Her friend had always been one to play the martyr, always taking burden best shared, solely onto her own thin shoulders. Every year, despite Sylvia's pleas otherwise, Greta's walnut carapace would harden, as the dread date edged closer. The first of December this year marked the fourth anniversary of the demise of Pevril Pudding; Greta's husband. Sylvia thought back to those early months of Greta's widowdom. What should have been a breath of fresh air and a clean start for her best friend was anything but. Did that brute slip quietly into the night? No. No he did not. Pevril Pudding had been a rough and hot-tempered sort in life, and it seemed that he kept his ill temper into the grave, and out again.

Sylvia had moved in a few months after his passing, taking up the box bedroom above the Toy Hospital, at the back, overlooking the yard and the alley that hid there. But even in death that oafish man liked to throw his weight around, though of course in his new situation, he was much less able to leave bruises as evidence.

As the first anniversary of his death had approached, bumps in the night grew bumpier, the things in the corner of their eyes became thingier, and the spooky shadows at their backs ever spookier! They could tell something was happening, they knew in their bones that something was coming.

That first year it was flies. Somehow a swarm of flies was conjured into Greta's bedroom, where they buzzed, thick as molasses around her head, trying to force their way into her nose and mouth. Shrieking and spitting, Greta had hid under her duvet, flailing and squirming, trying to seal herself up tight in the covers. She hid there wailing until the buzzing had ceased. Sylvia had come to the rescue armed with the bug zapper from the kitchen. As Greta's hair-netted head appeared cautiously from the safety of the covers, Sylvia switched off the glowing trap and sniffed, saying "I'll get a dustpan and brush."

The swarm was swept up and disposed of. Sylvia thought abstractly how the tiny dead bodies looked like raisins, until one of the little beasts twitched its wings, and she slammed the lid of the bin shut tight.

The next year was spiders. On the night of the first of December they wove a cocoon around poor Greta's bed while she slept; a million spindly, hairy legs silently tip tapped across the cotton sheets, weaving their own thick, sticky, smothering shroud. Sylvia had made sure to stay up late, in case of just such an eventuality. But she hadn't counted on spiders. Those wriggly, jiggly, creeping little creatures sent a shiver up her spine.

"Too many knees." She often said of spiders, "They move all wrong. Can't abide 'em."

But she had gulped down her fears, rushing to the aid of her best friend in all the world. A bread knife from the kitchen made short work of the smothering weave, from which Greta erupted like a fountain, gasping and spluttering, sweaty and with a harpy screech. The octopedal assailants scuttled away, vanishing between floorboards, under the skirting board, and away into shadows. That night, even a mug of hot cocoa hadn't soothed Greta's nerves enough to return to sleep. A week and a half she had slept on the settee in the living room. It hadn't done her back, or her temper, any favours.

"But how do you know it's Pevril's ghost?" Sylvia had asked a very peevish Greta, the following year.

"I just do!" Her friend said, grinding her teeth, hunched, and with folded arms, sitting behind the Toy Hospital counter. They were surrounded by the gaiety of their tinselled Christmas decorations, but feeling none of the cheer, "It's the stupid nursery rhyme he liked to sing at me."

"A nursery rhyme?" Sylvia was mystified. Though she had known a little of Pevril's cruelty, Greta never opened up a great deal, and this was new information, "He sang a nursery rhyme?"

"At me. If ever he found a dead fly, or a spider, or some such thing, wherever he was in the shop, he would creep up on me, singing that damnable ditty, and try to..." She paused, her teeth grinding like mill stones, "He'd try and feed it to me." That's how Greta broke yet another set of dentures.

Sylvia wondered what the song could have been that caused so much torment, and persuaded her dear friend that these odd yearly occurrences were the result of a hateful husbandly haunting.

"There was an old lady who swallowed a fly..." Greta said quietly, "I shan't say the rest out loud. I don't want to encourage the old blaggard."

Sylvia nodded, "It follows." She agreed, "Flies, spiders... then birds?"

Greta folded her arms, "Birds. Tonight I shall be Tippi Hedren."

"I was never fond of that film."

"I'm none too thrilled about reenacting it!"

And quell surprise she was not, when in the dead of night her bedroom window was flung open, and all manner of malformed and dirty pigeons beat their way inside. Greta found herself cut by claws, and the cold night air. She became entangled in crooked and twitching wings. In this grey storm of feathers and beady orange eyes she spun and wheeled, trying to find the door. They were in her hair, one got up her nightgown, and they obscured her vision. Unable to see which way was which, she stumbled toward the open window, and tripped on a bird flailing on the floor. A barren flower box saved her. Her hands landed upon it, and it fell in her place. It broke apart on the pavement below, scattering a rorschach blot of dark soil into the road. The birds fluttered over her head, pelting at one another and at her back with their moth-eaten wings to escape. They billowed as a cloud into the night sky, leaving Greta panting against the sil, dishevelled and cursing Hitchcock.

"How absurd, to swallow a bird..." Sang a horribly familiar voice at her back. Instinct took over and she spun around, raising her hands defensively. Pevril was not there... yet he was. A tarnished tin soldier, no bigger than a jar of jam, ran stiffly from the room, singing over its shoulder, "She swallowed the bird to catch the spider that wriggled and jiggled and tickled inside 'er!"

Fear, struck by Greta's iron hammer of will became rigid fury. She pelted after the toy as fast as her protesting hips and knees allowed. His rattling joints gave him away, as he shuffled awkwardly beneath the arm chair in the living room. She creaked just as loudly as she lowered herself to floor level, and peered under. Rattle rattle rattle! He was off and running again!

"She swallowed the spider to catch the fly!" He sang as he vanished through the living room door, "I don't know why she swallowed the fly..." and thud thud thud, down the stairs, "Perhaps she'll die!"

"Oh no you don't!" Sylvia said, out of sight. She had lain in wait for the night's shenanigans. There followed some banging and thrashing. Then, as Greta managed to lift herself upright again, the sturdy shape of Sylvia appeared at the door, wearing oven gloves, clutching a fishing net, and with a souvenir hat from Australia on her head, corks swinging madly on their strings.

"I missed." She said, "And he's vanished off into the shop somewhere. We'll never find him now."

Greta had forgone the cocoa that night and reached straight for the sherry. She stewed silently, grinding her false teeth, until fatigue overcame her and she began to snore. Sylvia tucked a thick blanket around her, and made sure there was a pot of tea ready the next morning.

"So..." Sylvia mulled over the jellicle connotations, "Tonight it's to be a plague of cats, is it?"

Greta stared across the crowded shop front, through the wonky window and to the brilliant gleaming snow outside. This year felt different. The snow storm, and her murderous ex-husband were somehow in cahoots. She knew it.

Pouring herself a second mug of tea, she sighed, "I've work to do, Sylv. All this hocum is nothing but a bother. This rocking horse won't mend its own leg, will it!"

"It's a little more than a bother, Greta! You've a ghost trying to finish you off with a nursery rhyme!"

THE NOVELTY HAS WORN OFF

Greta shooed her friend away, "Leave me be, you old fusspot."

Sylvia knew that when a conversation was ended by Greta Pudding, there was no resuscitating it. She left a handful of the tools from her jangling tabard pocket on the counter top, and shuffled away into the back room, where their kitchen was huddled in one dim corner. It was while she stood there, dunking a ginger-nut biscuit into her brew that an idea came to her. She smiled, and chortled a little, which gained her one very suspicious glare from Greta.

A few minutes later, biscuit and brew forgotten, Sylvia was off wading through the snow up Thomas Street on a mission. Greta watched her go, and shook her head. Her friend was prone to flights of fancy and whimsy. No doubt she would be regaled with a tall tale of city-centre adventure upon her return.

As her gaze lingered on the bright square of the front window, the pug and its owner made their way back the way they had come. Once more the little dog paused and cocked its leg.

Greta rushed forward, "None of that on my step, if you please!" She shouted through the glass of the door, startling the dog's owner.

Greta stewed behind the Toy Hospital counter, and found herself unable to focus on the lame rocking horse. The rickety thoroughbred was not due for collection until the following week, so she had time. It was simply something to do to occupy her mind. Yet it failed. Each time she picked up a tool, it wasn't the right one, or she couldn't quite get a good angle on the leg, or her back ached a little too much, or her knees demanded a rest. Furious, she threw down the tools.

"This just won't do at all!" She fumed at herself. Each year she became a hysterical mess, when beset by nursery rhyme beasts. Never before in her life had she ever screamed, or wailed, or even whimpered. Not even when Pevril was at his most vindictive and brutal. She was sensible, rational, dogmatic, pragmatic, and lots of other things folk said in hushed tones which she suspected weren't at all polite. Yet for the last three years, each December the first night, she had been reduced to a snivelling, skriking, shrieking shambles, "Not this year." She told herself resolutely, "And never again."

She did have two things to thank him for, that hateful dead husband of hers; the walnut shell inside which she dwelt, and the Toy Hospital itself. She closed her eyes, and forced her memories back, back, a long way back, to happier times. She did this whenever the weight of her wounds threatened to bury her, and smother her in melancholy.

THE NOVELTY HAS WORN OFF

As a marriage should start, theirs did; with love. Romance, and his strong arms both swept her off her kitten-heeled feet. She was quite the snappy dresser in her younger days. Pevril had been sent home from the early days of the War, lame. And the shy infatuation of their teenage years blossomed into lust and passion, and they were married on the seventh of September, 1940.

As they exploded together between the sheets, hot in each other's tight embrace on their wedding night, the Luftwaffe drummed a distant accompaniment across the south of the country. The beginning of the Blitz couldn't damage their passion, not even when it arrived on their doorstep and ruined Christmas that same year.

From Pevril's home in Oldham they could see the fires and smoke pouring from the city, a glittering spectacle, hellish and red, dramatic and terrible, red and shining like a dreadful festive bauble. Fires burned across Manchester, melting and gurgling, spitting and pluming; a volcano, an open wound, leading straight to Hell. Or so it seemed. But Greta was safe with Pevril. They danced around the living room every evening to their favourite records, safe and warm and occasionally well fed.

But the War following Pevril home had done something to him. Greta didn't see the sadness in his eyes, she ignored the trembling of his hands, finding comfort in his strong arms, as with her head pressed to his chest, they swayed and spun gently about the living room, night after night.

The bombs of her memory sounded suddenly loud and close, and she was snapped from her reverie by Sylvia's bustling return and the slam of the Toy Hospital door.

"It's quiet as the grave out there." She said, nodding over her shoulder, "Only a few places open. Looks like the snow has blocked all the roads and suchlike. No busses or trams or anything!" She hurried through the shop, leaving a trail of white footprints in her wake, at which Greta scowled.

"What have you got there?" Greta pointed a suspicious finger at the carrier bags slung over Sylvia's arm.

"None of your beeswax." Sylvia grinned, wagging a finger of her own, then vanished into the back room. Greta watched her go, and her gaze followed the sound of Sylvia making her way up the stairs to the first floor, and the click of her bedroom door closing.

"What's that daft mare up to?" Greta mumbled, before turning her attention to the rocking horse once more.

The hours trickled on, and by setting her mind to fixing the toys in her Hospital, she quite forgot about the impending attempt on her life. Until, that is, the little clock on the wall cuckooed seven in the evening. So absorbed in the plaining of a new rocker for the rocking horse had she been, that the day had quite passed her by. She nodded approvingly at her day's work, and allowed herself a rare smile. It was a pleasant and warm smile, as bright and lovely as her usual expression was frosty and pinched.

Standing up, she uncurled her spine, and groaned as it clunked in several places. She was prone to seizing up. Using her walking stick - which she hated to use - she made her creaking way to the front of the shop, flipped over the open sign to closed, and locked the door. As she made her way into the back room, she noted how bare and empty their little kitchen was. Sylvia would usually have it filled with dirty pans and the smells of some ungodly stew by now. But the oven was cold, and the pans sat clean in their cupboard. Across the very back wall, arching over the rear door and the kitchen cupboards were the open-sided stairs. Up this mountain trail she hiked, using the wobbly handrail and her stick for support, though she truly didn't ever feel much supported by either.

"I'll go rump over rumple down this staircase one day." She muttered to herself, looking back briefly to base camp.

"What did you say?" Sylvia's head appeared at the top of the stairs. Her cheeks were suspiciously rosy.

"Never mind that, what are you up to? You've no right looking so flushed, hiding away up here doing nothing."

"Ah but I haven't been doing nothing!" Sylvia helped to heave her friend up the last step, and into the narrow landing. There was a bit of business with elbows and bosoms, as Greta attempted to shuffle past.

"Mind where you're..."

"Oh sorry, here..."

"By heck!"

"Beg your pardon!"

"Do you want to know what I've been up to, up here *'doing nothing'*?" Sylvia said eagerly.

Eventually Greta navigated around her friend, and through her own bedroom door. She didn't want to linger, she didn't want to sit and chat in the living room as they usually did. She wasn't in the mood.

"Likely best I don't know." Greta said, but had some suspicions. She'd heard about ladies in their time of life suddenly finding new and strange hobbies. Exercise was one she found particularly troubling. All that jiggling about couldn't be good for you, she was sure of it.

THE NOVELTY HAS WORN OFF

"You want me to bring you a mug of cocoa, love?" Sylvia cooed.

"No. Thank you." Greta said as she disappeared from sight behind her bedroom door.

Sylvia sucked her cheek, concern written in bold print across her face. *Read all about it, read all about it!* She couldn't ever hide her emotions, or her thoughts. They blared out of her as a newspaper headline, for all to see.

She lingered there a moment, staring at the dark door, before returning to her secretive work. Presently, a loud scraping sound began to emanate from Greta's bedroom.

"Greta?" Sylvia tapped on the door, "Everything hunky dory?"

"As much as you'd expect, given the circumstances." Came the muffled reply.

"What're you up to?"

"Just shifting my furniture about. Having a little rearrangement."

"Feng shui?"

"...What did you call me?"

"No it's..." Sylvia gave up with the muffled conversation, "Never mind."

Greta was not indulging in a spot of evening Feng shui. No. Greta Pudding was building a barricade. In fact, she was building two. One across the door, and another across the window.

"See if you can get your mangy moggies in here now, you horrid little prick." She muttered as she strained, gritting her false teeth. The vanity went in front of the door, and the wardrobe in front of the window. The bed, with its solid metal frame and jangling springs was too much. She puffed and panted, sitting down heavily on her lumpy mattress. She wiped her brow with a handkerchief, and glared about her fortress.

"It'll have to do." She said.

That night she didn't sleep. She pulled up her duvet to make a warm tent for herself as she sat on the edge of the bed and waited. Her dry old muscles were taught like violin strings, and at any provocation she would emit a high C. The flutter of a pigeon alighting briefly on the window ledge startled her half to death. The creak of Sylvia's bed down the hall alarmed her again and again. Greta's ears strained for all sound, any sound, for a warning of what might be coming.

"I hate cats." Greta said to herself, "Pompous, entitled little beggars."

She wanted midnight to come, and for the terror to arrive and be done with. And midnight did come, eventually. She heard the clock downstairs cuckoo the hour. And nothing happened.

Greta realised she'd been holding her breath, and let out a long slow wheeze of relief. Had Pevril finally given up?

Crash! Bang! Wallop! Meaw!

The silence was smashed to pieces by the crashing of furniture, doors being slung roughly open, and a million hissing, mewing little voices. Greta let out an involuntary shrill squeak, and pulled her duvet tight about her. She expected her bedroom door to fly open, and the vanity to disintegrate under a thousand razor claws, and be caught in the headlamp glare of a billion yellow eyes! But the sounds that came crashing and bashing and smashing through the Toy Hospital slowed, faltered, and altered as they reached the landing, and her bedroom door. The hissing subsided. The vicious mewing became purring.

The chill of the night began to vibrate to the thrumm of a un unknowable number of purring cats.

Slowly, Greta relaxed her white knuckles, letting the duvet slip away. What was happening out on the landing? She rose from the bed, inching her way to the barricaded door.

"What have you done!"

Greta stepped back from the door as Pevril's voice broke through the white noise of happy cats.

In response to him, Greta heard Sylvia laughing, and then a series of clattering thuds, followed by a triumphant *'ah-ha'!*

"Sylv?" Greta called through the door, "Sylvia?"

Through the sound of contented kitties, she could hear metallic clinking and rattling.

"You can come out now, Greta. I've got him."

As a pale winter dawn rose over Manchester, Greta and Sylvia were sitting in their small living room, staring at a tin soldier in a bird cage.

"So…" Greta began. It had taken her a lot longer to remove the barricade than it had to put it in place, and she was very tired, "How did you…?"

Around them the carpet could not be seen, for the rolling, stretching, squirm bodies of cats. Black cats, tabby Toms, tortoise-shell moggies, mangy old creatures, spry little kittens. More even than T S Elliott could have dreamed up.

"Catnip." Sylvia said proudly, "I laced the stairs and landing with it."

That's the mission that had taken her into town earlier that day. A search for catnip. She had trudged through the snow, knee-high in some places, to every shop she could find that sold cat toys, food, and accessories. Everything with catnip in, she bought. She purchased Manchester's entire supply that day.

THE NOVELTY HAS WORN OFF

And back at the toy hospital, while Greta was downstairs grinding her teeth, Sylvia had set to work. She snipped open all the toys and trinkets, ripped open the bags, and ran seams of the stuff through the landing carpet, and around their bedroom door frames.

"I'm surprised you didn't notice the smell yourself, as you went up to bed." Sylvia chuckled.

"I did, in fact, notice it." Greta lied, "But I thought you'd been doing exercise or some similar unhealthy carry-on and that the aroma was you."

Greta was being very snippy. Probably from lack of sleep, Sylvia thought.

"Well once that was done, and you were to bed, all I had do was wait."

And Sylvia waited. She sat on her uncomfortable bed and fidgeted impatiently, with oven gloves on, her Australian souvenir hat jammed over her hair, and armed with a fishing net.

Midnight came, and Sylvia's eyes had fallen closed with boredom and she had begun to sleep. She woke abruptly to the crashing and bashing sounds of a tidal wave of cats rolling through the shop downstairs. The wave broke on the stairs, spraying raging balls of feline ferocity into the air. The landing was inundated in moments, and Sylvia gulped hard, clutching the net, as the maleficent moggies began to eye her up, stretching and extending their needle claws. But she needn't have fretted. It took them a few moments to notice the dreamy fragrance, and a few moments more to succumb to its heady powers.

Riding on the back of one of the larger Toms, Pevril kicked and punched at the tamed cats. Then, spotting Sylvia's red, laughing face he knew he was beaten.

"What have you done!" He cried at her, raising his stiff tin arms in the air in a rage.

The net came down on him swift as Sylvia could manage, and she bundled him up into a bag, which was then shoved into an old bird cage.

And that's where Pevril remained, as Sylvia recounted her tale. All the while, Greta stared daggers at the tin soldier, whose emotionless metal face glared back, somehow mocking her.

"What have you to say for yourself?" Greta asked, keeping as level a voice as she could manage through gritted dentures.

But Pevril said nothing.

THE NOVELTY HAS WORN OFF

Fambles – Year 3 Anthology For 2021

DAVID RICHARDS

Another year of socially distanced Fambles meetings.

Another year of uncertainty...

With vaccinations and booster shots, borders re-opening, foreign holidays resuming, rules relaxing, things are slowly getting back to some kind of normal.

Through it all, Fambles was there. Officially, once a month, but sometimes fortnightly, sometimes weekly, depending on how we felt. We would share our work, have a good old gossip, or sometimes just guzzle down lashings of wine and gin. It was a lifeline in a sometimes-frightening time.

I still haven't gotten back into my pre-pandemic rhythm and my output has been woefully lacking, but having Fambles has forced me to put pen to paper (or fingers to keyboard) and write, if only to make sure that I had something to read at the meetings. Without Fambles I have no doubt that my output for the last year would have been nil!

My first piece is the first chapter of my work in progress. It's a spin-off from my previous novel 'Bitches'. I hope to finish it very soon!

My second piece is a short story which, funnily enough, also features a couple of characters from

'Bitches'. I make no apologies. I loved writing that book and can't seem to let go of the characters just yet! I also have a feeling that we may be seeing a little bit more of Randall in the future.

My third and final piece is a few chapters from something that I started, put away, then pulled back out again. I liked it, it has a few old characters from some of my other books in it, and I'm not ready to give up on it! By including it here and sharing it with you, it's a reminder to myself to finish it!

THE NOVELTY HAS WORN OFF

WITCH HUNTERS

'Wakey wakey, almost there.'

Diana lay in the backseat of the car. As she came to, she watched as the lights from the streetlamps lit the roof, then plunged her into darkness for a second before lighting it up again.

The motion of the car combined with the strobing lights was making her woozy. She tried to sit up, but couldn't manage it. Puzzled, she wiggled her feet. They were bound together at the ankles. Her hands tied behind her at the wrists.

'Whaaa....?' She began.

'Oh, you're awake,' the driver said. 'Finally. That's good. I thought I might have given you too much. It wouldn't do to have you dying in the backseat, would it? Wouldn't be anywhere *near* as much fun!'

'Wazgoinon?' Diana slurred, wriggling about in the backseat trying to get free from her restraints.

'Oh, don't bother,' the driver said. 'It's not my first rodeo, this. You won't be getting loose until I want you to.'

Diana struggled to remember what had happened. She had been at the pub with her friends until, one by one, they had gone home leaving her by herself. She had ordered one more drink and...

Nothing.

THE NOVELTY HAS WORN OFF

That's where it all went blank.

'Trying to remember, are you?' the driver asked as if reading her mind. 'You should have gone with your friends. Don't you know that girls have been going missing? It's almost as if you *wanted* to be taken!'

His voice was familiar. Through the fug, she tried to remember, until... The barman. It was the barman.

'You're special, you know,' the driver continued. 'Not just any old victim. You're number twenty! Twenty! Can you believe it?'

Diana tried to scream but only managed a raspy croak.

'Oh, don't bother,' the driver said. 'There'll be lots of time for screaming later. You save your energy. You're going to need it.'

Diana wriggled about some more, testing the restraints, then gave up. It was no use.

'Lemmego,' she slurred. 'Please.'

'Bingo!' the driver said. 'That's twenty out of twenty. They've all said that one. I've had thirteen 'you don't have to do this', seven 'I've got a family', and two that said that they'd team up with me and help me lure more victims. Why don't you try for something original?'

'You're going to regret this,' Diana said. 'I promise.'

'That's five,' the driver said. 'Five of you have said that one. Here we are.'

The car slowed down and Diana heard the tyres crunch over loose stones and dried leaves. The car stopped and the driver shut off the engine.

'Now,' he said, taking off his seatbelt and turning to look down at her. 'I'm feeling generous tonight, seeing as you're so special. Usually, I give a ten-minute head start, but as you're number twenty, I'll give you twenty minutes. How does that sound?'

'Head start?'

'To run,' the driver said. 'You run and hide. If I don't find you, you get to live. If I do... Well, let's just say that I've found every girl so far. I'm very good at what I do. So! Twenty minutes. Starting from when I cut you free. Those are the rules. Got it?'

Diana nodded her head.

'Good girl.'

The driver got out of the car and opened the door to the back. He grabbed Diana's feet and pulled her roughly from the back seat. Her head bounced off the door jamb, then hit the ground. She groaned as the driver untied her feet, then he turned her onto her front and released her hands.

She struggled to stand, dazed from the blows to her head and the remnants of whatever he had slipped into

THE NOVELTY HAS WORN OFF

her drink. She steadied herself by holding onto the car's door and tried to take in her surroundings.

They were in the woods. In front of her was a dirt path that he had driven down, behind her were trees. Dense, dark trees.

'Yes,' the driver nodded. 'I'd go that way if I were you. Aim for the road and I'll catch you in no time. No traffic and no coverage. You won't be rescued and I'll see you from a mile off. Yes, I'd say that the woods were your best bet, but it's completely up to you. Tick tock.'

He tapped his wrist to let her know that her time was counting down.

'Why?' Diana asked.

'You want to waste time chatting?' The driver replied. 'You should be using every minute.'

'Why?' Diana asked again.

'Why not?' The driver asked. 'It's fun. It keeps me alert. It's cheaper than a gym membership. And there's no shortage of stupid bitches coming into the pub. It's easy to pick off the odd one.'

'You're sick,' Diana said.

'Thirteen out of twenty,' the driver said. 'Still nothing original. Go on. Run.'

Diana let go of the car door and staggered away

She bounced from tree to tree as she went deeper into the woods, the treetops forming a canopy and blocking out the moonlight so that she was running almost blind.

She carried on forwards, her mind clearing as she pulled in lungfuls of fresh air. She pushed on, the environment around her barely changing until she crashed through thick underbrush and found herself bathed in moonlight.

She was in a large clearing. Trees formed a circle around a smooth lawn, broken up by small mounds.

Diana walked over to one of the mounds, then gasped as she saw a skeletal finger poking out from the earth as if beckoning her to join it.

She took a step backwards as she counted the mounds. Nineteen. He was telling her the truth. She had found his burial ground.

Nineteen girls. All brought here and all killed here.

Diana shook her head. She wasn't going to be number twenty. She wasn't going to be one more mound in the middle of a wood. She wasn't...

'You made it!'

As Diana backed away, the driver emerged from the trees opposite her, carrying a large holdall. He sauntered past the mounds and stopped, dropping his bag in front of him and smirking at her as she walked backwards towards the trees.

'That wasn't twenty minutes,' Diana said. 'You said that I had twenty minutes.'

THE NOVELTY HAS WORN OFF

'I lied,' the driver said. 'And I wouldn't bother trying to run if I were you. I know these woods like the back of my hands.'

'Is that for me?' Diana asked, nodding at the bag. 'Ropes, knives, all that sort of stuff?'

'Clever girl,' the driver nodded. 'Only three of you have asked that. Usually, they're crying and blubbering round about now.'

'I won't cry,' Diana said. 'I won't give you the satisfaction.'

'Twelve out of twenty,' the driver said. 'And you will. You'll cry and you'll scream and you'll beg.'

'No, Ben,' Diana said. 'No, I most definitely will not.'

'You remembered my name!' Ben said, crouching down and unzipping his bag. 'Four out of twenty. Not that it matters. So, shall we get on? I'm thinking we'll start with the pliers and work our way up to the knives. Unless you have a preference?'

'I do,' Diana said. She had stopped backing away and was now walking towards Ben. 'But I don't think you have it in that bag.'

'Oh, I don't know about...' Ben began, then stopped as he saw Diana approach. 'Six out of twenty. You're going to try and overpower me. You can try. I quite like it when they get feisty. Come on. Give it your best.'

Ben stood back up and gestured for Diana to come at him. She stopped and smiled.

'I've no doubt you'd win if it were hand to hand,' Diana said. 'You're a big strong man and I'm just a defenceless little woman, after all. I had something else in mind.'

'Eight out of twenty,' Ben said. 'Offering me sex. Tedious.'

He took a step towards Diana then stopped as she pointed a finger at him. He looked at her in confusion, then tried to take another step.

His legs wouldn't move. His feet were rooted to the spot.

'What?' He asked. 'What's going on?'

'One out of twenty,' Diana said, pointing her finger towards the ground. Ben immediately sat down. 'Nineteen girls, one witch.'

'You...'

Diana swiped her hand to the right and Ben's mouth clamped shut.

'You saw a group of girls tonight,' Diana said, stalking around Ben as he sat, helpless and immobile. 'Drinking, peeling off one by one. Oh, we knew what you'd been up to. We knew you were ready for another night of hunting. We knew. I drew the short straw. I was to be the one that you took. *You* saw a group of girls. You were wrong. What you *actually* saw was a coven.'

Ben struggled to talk but his mouth remained tightly closed.

Diana swiped her hand again and Ben gasped for breath.

'One out of twenty,' Diana repeated. 'Is this original enough for you?'

'Please!' Ben gasped. 'Please, just let me go.'

'Ugh,' Diana said, rolling her eyes. 'Say something original! They *all* say that one. Fifty-seven out of fifty-seven. Why don't you make it a clean sweep and cry out for your mother, too?'

She held her arms up and formed two fists, then squeezed. Ben's legs were crushed, the bones shattering as he screamed in agony.

'I'll stop!' Ben screamed. 'I won't do it again!'

'Of *course* you won't,' Diana said, swishing her hand. A hole opened up in front of Ben and, as Diana slowly moved a finger in the air, he was dragged by an invisible force towards it. 'You're going to be staying here. *You're* going to be mound number twenty. You thought that you were going to be the hunter? Bitch, you were the prey!'

Fambles – Year 3 Anthology For 2021

THE NOVELTY HAS WORN OFF

WHO YOU GONNA CALL?

'Is he here?'

Betty dried her hands on a tea towel, then threw it to the side.

'He should be here by now,' she continued, going to the front door of the cottage where her daughter hopped from foot to foot, scanning the street.

'Not yet,' Sandra said. 'He's late. He said two and it's ten past, now.'

'These things happen, love,' Betty said. 'Folk get held up. Come on. Get sat down. He's not going to get here any sooner with you skenning up and down t'road.'

'As soon as I shut this door he's going to knock,' Sandra said. 'Mark my words. I'll just stay here. Go and do the washing up or summat. Make yourself useful.'

'It's done,' Betty said. 'I've been doing it for the past half hour, which you'd have noticed if you weren't bobbing about in that doorway like a constipated penguin.'

'He came highly recommended,' Sandra said. 'Best in the business, Lillian said.'

'I know,' Betty said. 'You've told me. Many, many times. Are you sure we need him, Sandra? Can't you just use your gifts? You keep telling me how powerful you are. Do we really need outside help?'

'He's not listening to me,' Sandra said. 'I've tried. I've told him to stop beggaring about with the taps, but he's not for having it. We need a professional.'

'Is this him?' Betty asked, pointing to a figure walking up the road. 'Ooh, isn't he dapper?'

The man wore a broad-brimmed hat, a long, black coat, and was tapping his way up the road with a silver-topped cane.

'Cooee!' Sandra called out, waving to the man. 'Cooee, over here, love.'

'Sandra!' The man said, tapping the brim of his hat with the cane. 'Nice to finally meet you in person. And this must be your mother. Betty, yes?'

'That's right, love,' Betty said. 'Come in. Let's get this over with.'

'What a lovely little cottage,' the man said as he walked through the door, handing Sandra his hat and coat. 'So rustic.'

'Thanks, love,' Betty said as Sandra hung up the man's garments. 'So, you're a ghostbuster, then?'

'Not quite,' the man said. 'Randall James, psychic investigator. At your service.'

'You can get rid of the bugger, though?' Sandra asked. 'Jack, he's called. Says he built this house in the sixteen hundreds. He's forever messing with the

THE NOVELTY HAS WORN OFF

taps. And lightbulbs! He's a bugger for lightbulbs. I'm a psychic medium myself, you know, but he's not listening to me. Won't leave. I think he's taken a shine to me.'

Randall took a good look at Sandra. Medium might be pushing it a bit, he thought, taking in her short, squat frame. She was definitely more of a large.

'I've tried everything,' Betty said. 'I've been smudging, chanting... He won't sod off. I haven't seen him meself but our Sandra's been going spare.'

'There's something here, alright,' Randall said. 'I can definitely feel a presence.'

He held up his hands and waved them about, turning slowly in a circle.

'What's he doing?' Betty asked. 'Is he dancing?'

'Just getting a feel for the place,' Randall said. 'You say you haven't seen him, Betty? I'm surprised. I feel a power coming from you.'

'Aye, well,' Betty said. 'I do have a bit of the gift. Nothing like our Sandra. We're thinking of starting a coven. Just me and Sandra, and maybe Lillian from work. She's a healer, she says. I'm not convinced. If she was, you think she'd have cleared up her dandruff by now.'

'Ah, Lillian,' Randall said. 'Yes, I know Lillian.'

'She's the one what recommended you,' Sandra said. 'When I told her about our little problem. You know, this gift? Sometimes it's a blessing but sometimes... *Sometimes* it's a bit of a curse. Well, I don't need to tell you, do I?'

'Where are my manners?' Betty asked. 'Do you want a brew, love?'

'I won't,' Randall said. 'I'd like to get straight into it if that's alright. The presence that I feel. It's not malevolent. I feel a sadness.'

'Well, no bloody *wonder*,' Betty said. 'You're not going to be full of the joys when you're a ghost, are you? Sadness, he says. They're hardly likely to be doing the can-can, are they?'

'Alright, mother,' Sandra said. 'Let him do his job.'

'And how much are we paying for this?' Betty asked. 'Or how much am *I* paying for this, I should say.'

'Shhh,' Sandra said. 'You'll put him off. It's very delicate work, this. You wouldn't understand.'

Betty tutted, but said nothing as Randall waved his hands about in the air. Sandra nodded sagely as Randall hummed and seemed to pluck at the air.

'Aye,' Sandra said. 'I know that one. I've tried all that.'

'Taps, you say?' Randall asked. 'And lightbulbs?'

'That's right,' Sandra replied. 'Dripping taps and flickering lightbulbs. Eeh, he's a bugger for lightbulbs. I was only just telling me mum.'

THE NOVELTY HAS WORN OFF

'Have you...' Randal began, then plucked at the air some more. 'Have you checked the fuse box? I'm getting that you might have a loose connection.'

'Ooh!' Betty said, impressed. 'Did Jack tell you that?'

'No, dear,' Randall said. 'It's just common sense. And for the taps, I think I'd check your washers.'

There was a loud, clattering sound and the three of them jumped.

'Did you hear that? Sandra asked. 'You must have heard that? Oh, that frightened the life out of me, that did. He's not happy, is he?'

'It's the letterbox, love,' Betty said, nodding towards the front door. 'It's just the post, you silly beggar. Tchoh.'

'Alright, ladies,' Randall said, rubbing his hands together. 'I can help you. Sandra, there is no Jack. I don't feel a masculine energy in this house at all. There is a presence that seems to be caught in the cottage, though. Betty, as the only other person here with some power...'

'Her? What about me?' Sandra asked. 'I'm the one with the power, you cheeky get. Ooh, I thought you were supposed to be a professional! You're getting it all skew-whiff, you are.'

'Betty,' Randall continued. 'Perhaps you could just give the presence permission to leave.'

'Aye, alright then,' Betty said. 'Go on. Bugger off out of it. Stop oining us and just move on.'

'I should be doing that,' Sandra pouted. 'You're not as gifted as me, mother.'

'Is that alright, love?' Betty asked Randall. 'Will that do it, do you think?'

'That should do it,' Randall said, waving his arms again. 'Yes, the spirit is able to leave. You'll have no more bother.'

'And how much do we owe you?' Betty asked. 'Just wait while I get me purse.'

'No charge,' Randall said, waving her off. 'I was coming this way, anyroad, and it hasn't taken me five minutes. Just leave me a good review online and we'll call it right. Sandra, my hat and coat?'

Sandra passed Randall his coat. As he shrugged it on, she threw his hat at him and opened the front door.

'Thanks a frig-load,' Sandra said as he left the cottage. 'You've been no help whatsoever.'

'What are you on about?' Betty asked. 'It feels a lot lighter in here now. Can't you feel it? No, love. Take no notice of her. She's just put out because you got rid when she couldn't.'

'Well,' Randall said. 'Have a pleasant d...'

Sandra slammed the door in his face, then turned to her mother, arms crossed.

THE NOVELTY HAS WORN OFF

'I'm glad I refused to pay him,' she said. 'Looks like you'll have to smudge the place again. Bloody charlatan.'

* * *

'You can go now, Hayley,' Randall said to the translucent young girl who walked beside him as they left the cottage. 'There's nothing keeping you here anymore.'

'I just thought I'd have a couple of minutes before I popped off,' Hayley said. 'I haven't been out of that cottage since I died there. Did you hear her? Sixteen hundreds? Load of shite. It was built in 1984!'

'You'd think she would have at least googled it,' Randall said. 'If you're going to be a fake medium, at least do your research!'

'Too lazy,' Hayley said. 'There's news articles she could have read. Even *I've* seen them! A 16-year-old dies in your cottage before you move in... You'd think she'd have known about that! I was used as a PSA for the dangers of underage drinking! Lazy fat tart.'

'She was a character,' Randall chuckled. 'I don't know why her mother encourages it. The things people will do for attention.'

'She's a fucking nightmare,' Hayley said. 'I've had to put up with her shite for years.'

'Well, it's over now,' Randall said. 'You don't have to put up with it anymore.'

'Oh, well,' Hayley sighed. 'Cheers for getting me out. I don't know what was holding me there, but I can go now. See what's next.'

Hayley waved goodbye to Randall, then shimmered and disappeared.

Randall's phone pinged. He pulled it out of his jacket pocket and swiped to the notification.

One new review. One star. One word.

'Fraud.'

'Fucking Sandra,' Randall said, shaking his head.

THE NOVELTY HAS WORN OFF

JUMBLE

Chapter 1

'That's the last of it,' Peter said, emptying the bin bag full of donated clothes onto the existing pile.

Viv, who had picked up a flimsy silk scarf from the pile, turned towards Peter. She daintily held the scarf across her mouth and moved her head from side to side.

'Am I enchanting you?' She asked, batting her eyelashes.

'You look like that bloody Sandra,' Peter said. 'Put that down before somebody sees you messing with the jumble.'

'Gypsy Macaroni,' Viv corrected him, tossing the scarf onto the pile. 'She'll give you a belt if she hears you calling her Sandra.'

'You know,' Peter said, gesturing towards the pile. 'I don't think I've ever seen so many tracksuits and dressing gowns in one place before.'

'All Primarni's finest,' Viv said. 'What were you expecting? They're donations from the parents of your pupils. It's hardly going to be designer gear, is it?'

THE NOVELTY HAS WORN OFF

'They're not *all* skint,' Peter told her. 'Some of the parents have a bob or two. They're just too tight to donate owt decent.'

'Just be grateful that they donated anything at all,' Viv said. 'Anyroad, even the minted ones can't be *that* minted. If they were, they wouldn't be sending their kids to a school in Millston!'

'Point taken,' Peter said. 'Right. We're done in here for now. Let's go through and tell Hitler and Eva Braun that we're finished. They might even let us go home!'

'Fat chance,' Viv said. 'We're not getting out of here until the tables are up, the jumble's sorted, and everything's set up to their satisfaction.'

Peter sighed and, balling up the now empty bin bag, opened the door to the main room of Roman Road community centre where everybody else was busy setting up for the next day's jumble sale.

As the door closed behind them, Viv grabbed Peter's arm to stop him.

'I'm glad to be out of that room, truth be told,' she whispered. 'It bloody STINKS in there!'

'I was going to say!' Peter whispered back. 'I thought you'd let one off! Honestly. You'd think they'd have washed their tat before donating it!'

'Ah, Peter. Viv. All done?'

Eileen strode towards the two of them, clipboard in hand, her glasses perched precariously on the end of her nose.

'Sieg Heil,' Viv whispered. Peter snorted out a laugh.

'I'm glad you're having fun,' Eileen continued, striking a line through "empty out donations" on her clipboard. 'It will make the day whizz by. Now, all the jumble has been deposited into the back, yes? Good. Now, if you could just pop back in there and sort it into piles that would be fantastic.'

'We *could*,' Viv said. 'But Peter has to make a phone call…'

'That's right,' Peter said, pulling his mobile from his pocket. 'I need to let Jayne…'

'That's Jayne "The Voice" Sparkle,' Viv interrupted.

'I need to let Jayne know that we've got the gin that she requested,' Peter continued. 'Got to keep the talent happy, haven't we?'

'Indeed, we do,' Eileen agreed. 'I must say, Peter. It's quite the coup to get somebody of her calibre to open our little jumble sale. We'll be packed to the rafters tomorrow! A local celebrity doing a good turn for her hometown. The press will eat it up! I don't know how you managed it, I really don't.'

THE NOVELTY HAS WORN OFF

'Yes, well,' Peter said, edging past Eileen and making his way towards the storeroom. 'I'll just pop in there and make my call. Won't be a tick.'

Viv began to follow him until Eileen barred her way with the clipboard.

'I don't think that it will take two of you to make a phone call, will it?' She asked.

'I suppose not,' Viv said, kicking herself for not thinking of a better excuse to get out of doing more work.

'No, I didn't think so,' Eileen said with a sharp nod. 'Off you go, then. That jumble won't sort itself.'

Viv grumbled and growled as she slowly made her way back into the prep room to sort through the donations.

She picked up a pink dressing gown from the pile and gave it a tentative sniff. With a grimace, she threw it back down. She regretted volunteering to help, but if it meant spending a few hours with Peter then she would just have to suck it up and get on with it.

She reached down and picked the dressing gown back up and began to fold.

Chapter 2

'Well, that's the problem with the younger generation, Father,' Eileen said. 'They've no work ethic. They'd rather be out drinking or happy slapping or whatever it is they get up to these days. That Viv, for example. She just tried to get out of sorting the jumble.'

'Hmmm,' Father Jude said, feigning interest. He snuck a glance at his watch and debated with himself whether it was too early for a quick sherry. He glanced towards the shutters of the canteen, willing Betty to open up so that he could get to the bottle he had hidden there earlier.

'I soon put paid to that,' Eileen continued. 'She's in there now. I'll send Jack through in a moment. He'll make sure that it gets done. It'll keep him out from under our feet, too.'

'Where's that Nancy-boy got off to?' Father Jude asked.

'Nancy-b... Do you mean Peter?' Eileen asked, looking up from her clipboard.

'Petra more like,' Father Jude said. 'Yes, him. Where's he buggered off to? Isn't he supposed to be helping her?'

'He's on a very important phone call,' Eileen said. 'Making sure that our celebrity guest is happy. We would never have been able to afford her usual fee but

THE NOVELTY HAS WORN OFF

Peter convinced her, don't ask me how, to do it for free! All she asked for was a case of gin!'

'Gin, you say?' Father Jude asked, perking up. 'We've got gin?'

'It's in the canteen and it's not for us,' Eileen said. 'It's for Jayne. Her rider, I think it's called.'

'Why's that Viv hang around him all the time?' Father Jude asked. 'She's not going to get owt from him. She's barking up the completely wrong tree with that one, the daft cow.'

'She's got a crush is all,' Eileen said. 'It's not harming anybody and she's a grown woman. She'll get over it. It's fine. Leave them be.'

'And him, a teacher,' Father Jude continued. 'With his affliction. He shouldn't be around kiddies with that. You know what it says in the bible about all that carry on, don't you?'

'Yes, well,' Eileen said. 'I'll just go and see how Sandra, sorry, Gypsy Macaroni is getting on.'

'Disgusting is what it is,' Father Jude said as Eileen walked away. 'I've a good mind to...'

Eileen tapped on the window of the reception booth, startling Jack who was flicking through a magazine. He stood up straight and snapped off a salute to Eileen.

'Can you go into the prep room and give Viv a hand?' Eileen asked him. 'Thank you, Jack.'

'Aye, aye,' Jack said, opening the door and stepping out of the booth. 'All set up in here, anyroad. Raffle tickets ready, entry fee sign prominently posted. I'll just have a quick word with Father Jude, then…'

'Now, please,' Eileen said. 'Go on. Quick sticks.'

Jack clicked his heels together, then strode across the main hall and into the prep room.

'Now, Sandra,' Eileen said, approaching Sandra's small table. She narrowed her eyes and peered through her glasses as she tried to read the sign that Sandra had placed in front of it. 'Everything alright, here?'

'It's Gypsy Macaroni if you don't mind,' Sandra told her, rubbing the crystal ball in the centre of the table with her sleeve.

'My apologies,' Eileen said. 'What's all this?'

Eileen gestured towards the sign.

'Just letting folk know what's what,' Sandra told her, pushing her tarot deck next to the crystal ball. 'They'll know they're going to get a top-notch reading if they see all my credentials before they cross my palm with silver.'

'Seventh daughter of a seventh daughter,' Eileen read. 'Born in a caul, able to part the veil… None of that is strictly true, though, is it?'

'Some artistic license has been taken,' Sandra agreed, adjusting her turban. 'But my gift is undeniable. Well, I say gift. Some days it's more of a curse.'

'I'm sure,' Eileen said, crossing "Fortune Teller" off her clipboard.

'What do you think of the turban?' Sandra asked, receiving a short nod from Eileen. 'I was going to go with a blonde wig, but I think I'm done with my Marilyn Monroe phase. She's stopped coming through, so sod her.'

'Right, well...' Eileen began.

'What's that?' Sandra asked the empty space to the right of Eileen. 'Yes, love. Yes. What was it? Tuberculosis? Yes, I'm sure your mother will be along soon.'

Eileen gave Sandra a puzzled look.

'Little lad. Seven years old,' Sandra explained. 'Looking for his mother.'

'Speaking of,' Eileen said, glad to be changing the subject. 'Where's your mother got to? Betty?'

'She's in the canteen,' Sandra told her. 'She's almost done setting up.'

As if on cue, the canteen shutters went up with a loud clatter. Father Jude shot over and nodded towards the counter. With a sigh, Betty reached down and brought up a bottle of sherry. She poured a small amount into a glass and passed it to Father Jude who knocked it straight back, placed the glass back on the counter and walked away.

Eileen crossed "Canteen" off her clipboard and went over to speak to Betty.

'All done in there?' Eileen asked.

'All set up,' Betty replied, moving Father Jude's used glass to the side. 'Everything's ready for tomorrow. Ooh, it's going to be champion. Here, do you reckon we'll make enough to get St Joseph's those computers? Those poor little kiddies at that school, it's like something from the 80s!'

'Well, with your Sandra…'

'Gypsy Macaroni,' Betty corrected her.

'… and her fortune-telling, plus all the jumble donations,' Eileen continued. 'Not to mention the raffle, the cakes and sandwiches plus the entry fees, we'll definitely be taking more than last year.'

'Oh, that is good,' Betty said, wiping her hands on a dishtowel. 'Although it wouldn't take much, would it? Not after…'

'But I think what will actually put us over the top is having a celebrity here,' Eileen said, cutting Betty off. 'We're going to charge for pictures. That alone should make us more than enough for a computer or two for the school.'

'She's a slapper that one,' Father Jude said, startling Betty and Eileen.

THE NOVELTY HAS WORN OFF

'Where did you creep up from?' Betty asked.

Father Jude ignored her question and pointed towards his glass, which she begrudgingly topped up with sherry.

'I beg your pardon, Father,' Eileen asked.

'Jayne Sparkle,' Father Jude said, taking his drink from Betty. 'I know her of old. Slapper.'

'Well, I'm sure I don't know anything about that,' Eileen said with a scowl. 'But slapper or no, she's doing us a huge favour.'

'That's your lot now, Reverend,' Betty said, pointing to Father Jude's glass. 'We don't want you coming in here tomorrow with a hangover.'

'It's Father, not Reverend,' Father Jude told her. 'As well you know. A little respect, if you don't mind.'

'Sorry, Reverend,' Betty said, throwing her dishtowel onto the counter and turning her back on him.

Father Jude took a sip of his sherry, then slowly made his way to the corner of the hall, nursing his glass as he went. He lowered himself into a plastic chair, then took another long sip of his drink.

Eileen swept past him, clipboard tucked under her arm, and reached for the handle of the door to the prep room.

Before she could grasp it, a bloodcurdling scream came from the room.

'That bloody Jack,' Father Jude said, angry that he had almost spilled his drink. 'Get in there, woman. Bugger only knows what he's doing to that poor girl.'

THE NOVELTY HAS WORN OFF

Chapter 3

Viv was throwing a small tantrum. She was alone in the prep room surrounded by donated clothes and she was fuming.

She stomped her feet and kicked at the pile. Feeling a little better she shook her fist at the clothes and muttered expletives at them. She was about to spit on the pile of clothes when Jack came into the room. He saw her doing what appeared to him to be a rain dance and gave her a knowing look.

'I know that one,' he told her. 'Oh, yes. Saw it when I served in the Congo.'

'You what?' Viv asked.

'The Congo,' Jack replied. 'When I was in the army.'

'What do you want, Jack?' Viv asked him, already tired of his presence.

'I've come to give you a hand,' Jack said. 'Eileen's orders. I think she knows that a military man will have this lot shipshape and Bristol fashion in no time.'

'Alright,' Viv said, a little relieved that she wouldn't have to tackle the pile alone. 'I've folded that dressing gown and that's it. How shall we go about it?'

'Oh, no lass!' Jack said. 'I can't do anything too physical, not at my age. Too many old injuries. Can't risk it. No, I'll supervise. I'd start by sorting things into piles. Pants, tops...'

Viv reached down and, grabbing handfuls of clothes, started to throw them towards Jack.

'Woah, Woah,' Jack said, holding his hands up. 'I surrender. We come in peace. Slow it down, lass! You can't go chucking stuff around like that. We've got to sell this stuff. Think of the kiddies! When my old platoon stormed...'

'What's that?' Viv asked, nudging at the pile of jumble with her foot, cutting off Jack's tale.

'What's what?' Jack asked, standing next to Viv and peering down at the pile, unable to make out what it was that Viv was looking at.

'That, there,' Viv said, pointing to the floor.

Viv crouched down and grabbed what she had been pointing at. With a furrowed brow she gave the mysterious item a yank.

Jack stared, wide-eyed with shock, as Viv realised what she was holding onto. She dropped it to the floor and let out a bloodcurdling scream.

THE NOVELTY HAS WORN OFF

Chapter 4

Peter was the first to run into the prep room. He had been playing on his phone in the storeroom when he had heard Viv's scream and, without a thought, ran straight to her. He was closely followed by Eileen and Father Jude.

Betty and Sandra were the last to arrive. Betty gasped for breath, unused to moving so quickly, as Sandra looked around the room trying to figure out why Viv had been screaming.

'What is it, you stupid girl?' Father Jude demanded. 'Did Jack nip your arse or something? Get over it. Far too touchy these days. Your problem is you can't take a compliment.'

'I didn't lay a hand on her!' Jack protested.

'That!' Viv said, pointing to the floor. 'I was screaming at *that*!'

The group looked to the floor. Sandra gasped and covered her mouth with her hand.

'What is it?' Betty asked. 'I can't see without my specs and I've left 'em in t'kitchen.'

'I think we may have a slight problem,' Eileen said.

'That's a bloody understatement,' Father Jude said.

'What is it?' Betty asked again.

'It's a body,' Peter told her, stepping around her and putting his arm around Viv's shoulders to comfort her. She rested her head on his shoulder, still upset about finding a body under a pile of unsorted jumble but happy to have an excuse to snuggle up to Peter.

'A body?' Betty asked, her hand flying to her chest. 'Oh, no! They'll shut us down! They'll cancel the jumble and all them poor kiddies won't get their computers.'

'Who is it?' Jack asked. 'Do you want me to identify the corpse? When I was in Fallujah...'

'I'll do it,' Eileen said, pushing her glasses back on her nose and crouching down to the exposed arm. She started to move the garments away until she could make out a face. She recoiled with a gasp.

'Who is it, then?' Sandra asked.

'Don't you already know?' Viv asked her. 'I thought you had the sight.'

'If they're freshly deceased, they might not have got their bearings yet,' Sandra said. 'They'll speak to me as soon as they're able, I've no doubt.'

'Oh, I'm picking something up,' Betty said, holding her hand to her forehead and scrunching her eyes closed. 'It's a man... He's saying something about bumble... JUMBLE! That's what he's saying. Oh, I think it's the body.'

'Shut up, mother,' Sandra snapped. 'You're not getting a message from beyond.'

'Not from this one, anyway,' Eileen said, standing up and clutching her clipboard tightly to her chest.

THE NOVELTY HAS WORN OFF

'It's not a man. It's a woman. It's Angela. Angela Bodé.'

'The manager?' Jack asked. 'Bloody hellfire. Who'd kill Ange? Bugger! Will I be out of a job?'

'Somebody's strangled her,' Father Jude said, nodding towards the body. A pair of black leggings was wound tightly around her neck.

'Well, it wasn't me!' Viv said. 'I found her. I think I need counselling.'

'Pull yourself together,' Father Jude told her. 'There. You've had your counselling.'

'We need to call the police,' Peter said, pulling out his phone.

Eileen slapped it out of his hand. To Peter's relief, it landed on top of the pile of clothes.

'What the bugger do you think you're doing, woman?' Peter asked her, picking his phone back up and inspecting it for damage.

'Yeah,' Viv said, squaring up to Eileen. 'How *dare* you strike my boyfriend?'

'How many times?' Peter asked her. 'I'm not your bloody boyfriend!'

Viv shushed him as Eileen took charge of the situation.

'Let's think about this rationally,' Eileen said. 'If we call the police now, they're going to be all over the place with detectives and forensics and goodness knows what else. We can say goodbye to our jumble sale. As Betty just pointed out, they'll shut us down.'

'So, what do you suggest?' Peter asked. 'We hide the body? I'm not doing that. It's a crime!'

'You're not too fussy about committing crimes against the lord, are you lad?' Father Jude asked. 'Oh, no. You're quite alright with *that* when it suits. Disgusting.'

'Just what are you implying?' Peter asked Father Jude. 'You've been sniping at me for as long as I've known you. Go on then, *FATHER*. Spit it out. What's your problem?'

'You know full well what my problem is,' Father Jude said with a sneer. 'You'll have to answer to a higher power than me one day, my boy. And he won't be as merciful as I've been. Mark my words.'

'Oh, piss off,' Peter said.

Father Jude, unaccustomed to being spoken to in that manner, almost dropped the glass of sherry he was still clutching.

'Can we get back to the matter at hand?' Eileen asked. 'She's still warm. Whoever committed the crime is in this room.'

'It wasn't me!' Viv repeated. 'Oh, I can see you all looking at me. I know what you're thinking. You're all thinking just because I'm the pretty one that I'm a

THE NOVELTY HAS WORN OFF

femme fatale. Some sort of scarlet woman. Well, you can sod off right now. I'm not going down for this!'

'Pretty?' Sandra scoffed. 'You think you're pretty?'

'I could have been a model,' Viv insisted. 'If I hadn't chosen to become a receptionist at Peter's school, I could have been on the cover of...'

'The only thing that you could have modelled is balaclavas, love,' Sandra said. 'Cover up that face of yours.'

'You...' Viv broke away from Peter and lunged towards Sandra. Peter grabbed her and held her back as Sandra smirked at her.

'Take no notice of her,' Jack said. 'You're a very handsome woman, you are. You put me in mind of a slightly older Eva Peron. Now *there* was a woman. When I was in Argentina...'

'Back to the matter at hand, if you don't mind,' Eileen said. 'One of you in this room is a murderer...'

'Us,' Peter corrected her. 'One of *us* is a murderer.'

'It wasn't me!' Eileen said.

'Well, it wasn't me, either,' Peter told her. 'But you can't just leave yourself out. You're as much of a suspect as the rest of us. Even more so, I would say.'

'And why is that?' Eileen asked him.

'Really?' Peter asked in return. 'You *really* want me to say? Here? In front of everybody?'

'Yes!' Sandra exclaimed. 'Tell us! Oh, I knew she wasn't as buttoned up as she made out. I could see it in her aura.'

'Look,' Eileen said. 'Angela... Ms Bodé has very recently been murdered. The only suspects are in this room. What I propose is, we solve this mystery ourselves and *then* call the authorities. That way, we can hand the culprit over along with the body and there will be minimal disruption to tomorrow's jumble sale.'

'You're mad!' Peter said, making his way towards the prep room door. 'I'm leaving. I'm calling the police and letting them deal with it. Jumble sale be buggered.'

'Jack, stop him!' Eileen said.

Jack grabbed Peter, who struggled to break free but was surprised at the old man's strength.

'Alright, fine,' Peter said, giving up. 'We'll do it your way.'

Eileen gave Jack a nod and he released his hold on Peter.

'So,' Eileen said. 'I suggest we all make our way back into the main hall and we go from there.'

'Oh, isn't it exciting?' Betty asked Sandra as they left the prep room. 'It's like a Mrs Marbles or summat!'

THE NOVELTY HAS WORN OFF

ABOUT THE AUTHORS

Paul Magrs

Paul Magrs brought out his first novel in 1995 when he was 26. He has lectured in Creative Writing at UEA and at MMU. In 2019 he published his book on writing, 'The Novel Inside You'. In 2020 Snow Books republished his Brenda and Effie Mystery series of novels. In 2021 Harper Collins published his book of cartoons, 'The Panda, the Cat and the Dreadful Teddy.' He lives and writes in Manchester with Jeremy and Bernard Socks.

Jeremy Hoad

Jeremy Hoad lives in Levenshulme with his partner Paul Magrs, He founded and organises Levenshulme Pride which is now the largest free Pride in Manchester. He is also Chair of the Friends of Manchester's Gay Village to help make the Gay Village the best it can be. He has discovered a taste for activism and campaigning in recent years and stood as an independent candidate in the local elections this year.

Rylan John Cavell

Rylan is a tattoo artist and author, who is desperately trying to say goodbye to his regular-boring-day-job, and take up the arts full time! He'll get there one day! He is a playwright & author, was Original Fiction Editor for Starburst Magazine, and host and producer of The Gay Agenda radio show on Fab Radio International, and That's Pride on That's Manchester TV. He gave up on a career in media, much preferring to create art and write.

Find him online here:
www.rylanjohncavell.com

David Richards

David Richards lives in Manchester with his husband and two Pomeranians, Rula and Jinkx.

He has published six novels, all set in a fictional Northern town.

He is still very much a burden to his long-suffering husband, is still writing full-time, and is currently working on a new novel.

You can find his work on Amazon.

Fambles – Year 3 Anthology For 2021

THE NOVELTY HAS WORN OFF

Fambles – Year 3 Anthology For 2021

Printed in Great Britain
by Amazon